MASTERS OF SILENCE

KATHY KACER

annick press
toronto + berkeley

Cover art/design by Wenting Li/Kong Njo
Edited by Barbara Berson
Designed by Kong Njo

Annick Press Ltd.

We acknowledge the support of the Canada Council for the Arts and the
Ontario Arts Council, and the participation of the Government of Canada/
la participation du gouvernement du Canada for our publishing activities.

ONTARIO ARTS COUNCIL
CONSEIL DES ARTS DE L'ONTARIO
an Ontario government agency
un organisme du gouvernement de l'Ontario

Cataloging in Publication

Kacer, Kathy, 1954-, author
Masters of silence / Kathy Kacer.

(Heroes quartet)
Issued in print and electronic formats.
ISBN 978-1-77321-262-3 (hardcover).–ISBN 978-1-77321-261-6 (softcover).–
ISBN 978-1-77321-264-7 (HTML).–ISBN 978-1-77321-263-0 (PDF)

   I. Title.

PS8571.A33M43 2018   jC813'.54   C2018-904333-4
                                        C2018-904334-2

Published in the U.S.A. by Annick Press (U.S.) Ltd.
Distributed in Canada by University of Toronto Press.
Distributed in the U.S.A. by Publishers Group West.

Printed in Canada

www.annickpress.com
kathykacer.com

Also available in e-book format. Please visit www.annickpress.com/ebooks.html
for more details.

For Aura, Mannie, Raefie,
Viv, Sandy, and Allan—
my wonderful in-laws!

—K.K.

CHAPTER 1

April 1940

Helen

The heavy convent door closed behind her with an echoing thud, and Helen found herself standing in a cavernous hall as cold and nearly as dark as the streets outside. She could hear the steeple bell ringing, and she counted twelve loud clangs—midnight. Three nuns stood before her, moving their eyes slowly from her head down to her feet and back again. Helen coughed nervously and placed her small brown suitcase on the floor beside her. Then she removed her hat, smoothing down her short curls.

"How old is she?" the tallest of the three asked, leaning forward. She had a long, narrow face with dark eyes that Helen felt were staring right through her. She shrank back from her gaze.

"Fourteen," Helen's mother replied softly. "And very mature for her age."

"And the boy?" The nun stood back up and pointed in the direction of Helen's brother.

"Henry is ten." Maman stroked his head as she said this. Henry had begun to cry, his sobs echoing noisily off the stone walls of the convent. It was as if he knew what was coming and was dreading it all at once. "He's small for his age, but very smart, and also very responsible," she added. "It's just that he's tired. We all are."

Helen shuddered. Everyone was so somber. It made her feel even more afraid than she already was. The journey from Germany to here in southern France had taken days—Helen had lost count of how many. And they had barely seen sunlight in all that time; Maman had insisted that they travel mainly at night, walking long hours, and had only accepted a ride once, in a truck with the kind farmer whose wife had clucked sympathetically when she had seen Helen and her younger brother.

"It's good that they both have blond hair," the nun continued, studying the children with pursed lips and crossed arms. "It will make it easier if there are ever any questions."

Helen knew what that meant—the part about being blond. It meant that she and her brother didn't look too Jewish, like some of her friends who had dark hair, dark eyes, and prominent noses. These days, looking Jewish was not a good thing.

"And it's good that they both speak French," the nun continued.

Maman had been born in France and spoke only French to Helen and Henry. They had grown up listening to her stories about her childhood in Paris. Papa had spoken German to them, and Helen could move between the two languages as easily as she could switch from walking to running.

At the thought of her father, Helen shuddered again and squeezed her eyes tightly so that she wouldn't start to cry. How long had it been since she'd seen Papa? Perhaps more than a year! She could never forget the day he had been arrested and taken from their home in Frankfurt. It was seared into her memory like a deep scar. Nazi soldiers had run through the streets, smashing the windows of stores and synagogues, setting fires and attacking Jewish men and women who were walking outside, *just minding their own business*. There had been sounds of gunfire on the streets and people screaming. Papa had locked the door to their home and the four of them had stood together in a corner, clutching one another desperately, as if standing together could keep them safe. But a locked door meant nothing to the soldiers, who had smashed through it like it was paper, barged in, grabbed Papa, and took him away. It had happened in a moment—right before Helen's eyes—and she'd had no chance to say good-bye.

"He won't be any trouble, will he?" the nun asked. Henry was continuing to cry, his echoing wails growing louder.

"He'll be fine," Maman said. Her voice sounded strained and not at all convincing, at least not to Helen's ears. "It may take some time, but he'll settle," Maman added. She looked pleadingly at Helen, who moved over to put her arm around her brother. He looked so small and helpless, she thought. But even though she was trying to act like a helpful older sister, she felt just as defenseless.

"If he can't adjust, he may have to go somewhere else," the nun said.

Maman's eyes grew round with fear. "But there is nowhere else," she whispered.

After Papa had been taken, Maman knew they weren't going to be safe staying in their home. The soldiers had arrested only Jewish men, but Maman had said, "Families like ours may be next." And so they had packed a few things and left for the town of Kronberg, not far from Frankfurt. Maman knew a Catholic family who lived there, the Webers. Frau Weber had once worked for Papa, and she and her husband were willing to take them in. And there they waited for things to get better. But instead, everything had gotten worse. Adolf Hitler, "the evil one," as Maman called him, declared more restrictions against Jewish citizens. Orders, proclamations, rules, laws; they all meant the same thing—Jews couldn't do anything that others could do. And they could even be arrested if they were discovered, especially if they were found to be hiding with a Christian family.

After a while, Frau Weber spoke to Maman. "We're willing to let you stay, Frau Rosenthal," she had said. "We can say you are a servant here in the house. But the children ..." She glanced at Helen and Henry as she spoke, lowering her voice and moving closer to Maman. "If our home were searched, it would be impossible to explain why they're here. It's not that we wouldn't like to help. We would. What Hitler is doing to the Jews ... it's dreadful. But you must understand that it's terribly dangerous for us to protect all of you." That part was true. Christian citizens were in danger of being punished if they helped their Jewish friends and neighbors.

It was actually Frau Weber who had told Maman about the convent in southern France—a place that took in Jewish children without asking many questions. The next thing Helen knew, Maman was packing a few things for her and her brother, and they were on their way.

Helen looked over at the three nuns. The tall one who had done the talking was clearly in charge. The one on her left had a kind face that reminded Helen of Frau Becker, her teacher back in Frankfurt when she and her Jewish friends had still been allowed to attend school. When Helen looked at her, the nun smiled, and her eyes lit up and crinkled in the corners like a fan being folded up. But the nun on the right looked as if she already hated Helen, even though she didn't even know her. Her nose was scrunched up, and she pressed a tissue against it as if there were a bad smell in the room.

The tall nun was saying something else. "Do they have documents?" she asked. That's when Maman reached under her blouse and into the waistband of her skirt, pulling some papers out and handing them over to the nun.

"I didn't want anyone to find these," she said. "These are their identity documents." As she handed the papers over to the tall nun, Helen could just make out the red letter J that was stamped on each of their papers—the letter that meant that they were Jewish, the letter that had forced them to be on the run.

It was still so confusing to Helen: Why was being

Jewish was such a terrible thing? Why had people gone from being kind to being cruel? Why had Papa been taken, along with so many others? Why? Why? Why? None of it made any sense.

"It's time to say your good-byes." The tall nun was talking once more. "We will take over from here."

Good-bye? Helen's heart began to beat hard in her chest and she suddenly felt light-headed, like the time she had almost passed out after cutting her knee on some glass and seeing the blood. She bit her lower lip and swallowed hard, trying to steady herself. Then she watched as her mother first bent to talk to Henry.

"You must be very brave," Maman said. She reached out to hug him. He clung to her so hard that the tall nun had to untangle his arms from around Maman's neck. That made Henry cry louder. He screamed out for her to stay and struggled to pull free of the nun, who continued to hold his arms. And then suddenly, he fell silent and went limp as a rag doll. His chin fell to his chest, and his shoulders slumped forward. Helen thought it was almost worse to see him this way. Shouting and begging had meant that he was fighting. Now he looked like a broken animal.

Maman's face was grayer than ash by the time she came to Helen and placed both hands gently on her shoulders. "Take care of your brother," she said. "You'll need to rely on one another from now on."

At first, all Helen could do was nod. She was afraid that if she said anything, she would break down. Instead, she reached up and placed her hand against Maman's cheek. Her mother pressed her own hand over Helen's and closed her eyes. "Where are you going to go?" Helen finally croaked out.

"Back to Kronberg," Maman said. "I'll wait there for news of your father."

"Why can't we wait with you?" Helen knew the answer even before she asked.

Maman sighed; she had answered this question many times on their journey here. "You know I can't protect you out there," she replied.

If Maman was trying to protect her, then why did this feel like a punishment? Helen wondered. And for what? She had done nothing wrong. She glanced over again at the tall nun, still holding Henry by the arms. She, too, wanted to scream and beg Maman not to leave them behind. But she knew it would do no good. Instead, she asked, "When will you come back?"

Maman shook her head.

That's when the tall nun cleared her throat. "It's best that you go, Madam Rosenthal," she said. "Lingering only makes it harder."

Maman sighed again. Helen stared intently at her mother's face, trying to memorize every detail: the brown freckle close to the side of her mouth;

her cheekbones, so high and round that they looked like small apples; her one eyebrow that always lifted higher than the other; her full, red lips. She knew she would need this mental image to draw on in the days to come. Maman stared back, first at Helen and then at Henry, as if she, too, were memorizing her children's faces.

"I love you both very much," Maman said. "Never forget that."

Finally, she opened the convent door and stepped outside. She looked to the left and to the right. And then, with one last backward glance at Helen, she disappeared into the darkness, and the convent door once again closed with a thud.

CHAPTER 2

Henry

Henry and his sister followed one of the nuns down a long hallway. Her black shoes peeked out from under her long black robe, and her steps sounded like steady drumbeats on the shiny wooden floor. She had introduced herself as Sister Cecile. She had a kind face, Henry thought, not like the tall nun who had done all the talking when they had first arrived—the one who seemed to be in charge. That one had a face like the crow that used to sit on the high wire next to their house in Frankfurt: a long, pointy nose and dark, sharp eyes that sat deep in their sockets. Her eyebrows were so thick and bushy that there was barely any space between them—like a mustache had been glued to her forehead. He might have laughed out loud if he wasn't so scared.

He kept seeing Maman's face, so pale and upset. It had terrified him to see her so worried, especially when he knew that it was all his crying and yelling that made her look that way. Her lips quivered as if she might cry. In his whole life, Henry had only seen her do that once before—the night Papa was taken. But Henry couldn't stop himself. He had thought that maybe, if he screamed long enough and loud enough, she would take him from this strange and spooky place. She would say, "Henry, my love, it's all a mistake. You're staying with me."

But instead, Maman had bent over him to say good-bye. She told him to be strong like Papa, and brave. He didn't feel strong and he certainly didn't feel very courageous.

"I have to stay in Kronberg to wait for news of Papa," Maman had said, but Henry didn't want to hear her say those things. Why did she get to leave this place while he had to stay behind? He struggled to cover his ears with his hands. Oh, if only the nun with the crow's face had let him go. But she had held his arms tight as he twisted first to the left and then to the right.

Papa would never have left him behind like this. He would have found a way to keep everyone together. His father was the strongest and smartest person that Henry knew. He remembered the times his father had lifted him high into the air and set him on his shoulders, carrying him around as easily as if he were a bag of feathers, saying, "One day, you'll be this tall, my boy!" Henry dreamed of growing as tall as his father—or taller. Up on Papa's shoulders, he felt as if he could see the whole world. Now, it felt as if every part of his world was disappearing faster than it took for snow to melt in his hand.

Papa would have fixed everything, Henry thought. He could do that—at least, that was what he had always done in the past. But Papa hadn't been able to fix the laws that said Henry couldn't go to the park, or ride his bicycle, or go to school. No one could change that, no matter how strong or smart or tall they were. And then, Papa had been arrested by those soldiers who wore dark uniforms and shiny black boots. They had armbands with that ugly black and red badge, the same sign that he'd seen on the flags that were everywhere in Frankfurt. These soldiers had grabbed Papa right in front of his eyes, and marched him away. And everything had gotten even worse.

Sister Cecile interrupted his thoughts. "All the

children sleep in these rooms," she said, pointing to the big wooden doors that they passed on the left and right. Helen tried to put her arm around his shoulders, like she had done before Maman left. Normally, that would have been fine, but not this time. Henry yanked his body away from her and watched her face fall. He didn't mean to hurt her feelings, and he didn't really know why he had pulled away from her. All he knew was that he wanted Maman, not his sister!

Suddenly, Sister Cecile came to a stop before one of the doors. It creaked loudly as she pushed it open and turned to face Henry. "This is where you will be sleeping, young man."

Henry slunk down into his shoes and moved to hide behind Helen, forgetting that a moment earlier, he hadn't wanted her to touch him. The small suitcase he was carrying thumped across his legs.

"Don't be afraid," the nun continued. She smiled as she said this, but that didn't make Henry feel better.

"Your sister will be sleeping nearby—just down the hallway and around the corner," Sister Cecile added.

Her voice was soft, like she was trying to calm him down, but his mind was tumbling even more. When they had been living with the Weber family in Kronberg, after Papa was taken, he and Helen had shared a room with Maman. Even though it was tiny and cramped, he liked that they had all been together. Now, Papa was gone, Maman had left, and his sister would not be with him. He remained hidden behind her.

"Can't we stay together?" Helen asked the nun, as if she had read his mind. "We don't mind if we have to share a room."

But Sister Cecile shook her head. "I'm afraid not. Girls with girls and boys with boys." She bent toward Henry. "There are boys your age in this room. Perhaps you'll make some new friends. Wouldn't that be nice?" she asked. "To make friends?"

Henry shrunk back even farther. He opened his mouth to say something and then stopped. He had tried begging Maman to stay, but that hadn't worked. He had screamed for Papa, but his father had not come back. There was no use yelling anymore, he thought. It was better to say nothing, not even to this kind nun.

Sister Cecile sighed and stood up. "You won't be far from your sister," she added. "Just a few rooms away." She pointed down the hall into the darkness.

That's when Helen bent down to him and brushed the curly bangs off his forehead. This time he didn't pull away. He didn't move at all. At first his chin stayed glued to his chest. Finally, he raised his head to stare at her.

"It's okay," she said. "You're going to be okay. We both will."

Please stay with me, Henry's eyes begged her.

"I'll see you in the morning," Helen continued. Henry knew she was trying her best to sound cheerful and positive. She looked to Sister Cecile and the kind nun nodded.

"Yes, you'll see each other tomorrow," the nun said.

Helen turned back to Henry. "I promise."

As she stood up, Henry grabbed her hand and squeezed, hard.

"Say something, Henry," Helen pleaded. "Please talk to me." But instead, he hung his head again and let go of her hand. It felt as if something inside of him had died, dried up like a plant that had been yanked from the soil. Helen sighed deeply. Sister Cecile picked up Henry's suitcase, and then took him by the shoulder and guided him into the dark room.

CHAPTER 3

Helen

Helen awoke almost more tired than when she had put her head down on the pillow. She had barely slept the entire night, tossing and turning in a waking dream of Maman and Papa, of the home she remembered in the good times. On most mornings, Maman would be making breakfast by now—eggs for Helen and Henry, and for Papa, salted herring and cheese that smelled so strong it would make Helen's eyes water. But maybe, if Helen was lucky, Maman would also bake fresh croissants, the kind she remembered from her own childhood in France. She would serve those warm, with butter that melted the second it touched the flaky pastry. Papa would be getting ready to go to his office. Even though, like other Jewish professionals, he was forbidden from working, he still offered his services to Jewish friends and neighbors. Any minute now, Maman would call up to Helen and Henry to get up and get ready for school. It usually took two calls before Helen would roll out of bed and get dressed.

Those memories were fresh in Helen's mind, even though it had been such a long time since she had shared mornings with her entire family. Now her father was gone—who knew where. There was talk of enormous prisons, some the size of villages, terrible places far away where Jews were being tortured. Maman refused to say much when Helen asked. All she said was that they must hope for Papa's safe return. But that hadn't happened. And now Maman, too, had disappeared in the night. Tears pooled in Helen's eyes and she wiped at them furiously. She didn't want to cry. She had to be strong for whatever she was facing here.

There was a bell ringing in the distance, and sunlight poured in from several large windows that extended across a long wall. It had been pitch-black when she had crept into this room the night before. Sister Cecile had shown her to her bed, and where to put her things. Before leaving her, Sister Cecile had whispered, "He'll be fine. I've seen so many others arrive here just like your brother. They all adjust eventually. They have no choice."

Helen hoped that was true. But she worried about Henry—worried that he had become quiet. She knew what he could be like when he was scared, how he could shut down—like the time that boy in his class had shoved him to the ground and grabbed his bicycle from him, saying, "Jews can't have these!" Henry had walked home, bruised and shaking. He didn't talk for days after that, no matter how hard everyone encouraged him. And that was over a bicycle! This time, Henry had lost Maman and Papa. She didn't know how or when he'd recover from that.

She sat up in her bed and looked around. In the early morning light, she could see eight cots lined up across from each other, feet pointing toward the center of the room. This place reminded Helen of the book she had read a year earlier. It was called *Madeline*, the story of a girl in an orphanage.

In an old house in Paris that was covered in vines,
lived twelve little girls in two straight lines.

Helen had practically memorized the whole thing. The girl in the book seemed to like the place she was living in. The nuns there were kind and the other children became her friends. Helen wondered if she would have the same experience here. All around her, girls were stretching, sitting up, and glancing around, seeing Helen for the first time. She pushed back the covers and swung her legs over the side of the bed.

"You're new." A girl sat up in the bed next to Helen's. She appeared to be about her age. She had long, wavy hair that was held back in a ponytail. Strands of dark curls that had escaped in the night hung in ringlets across her cheeks. She brushed them behind her ears as Helen nodded. "I must have really been sleeping when you came in," the girl continued. "Usually, I wake up when a new one arrives."

New one. Is that what she was?

"I'm Michelle," the girl continued.

"Helen," she replied softly.

"I know, it's hard to be here, right?" Michelle said. "Do you know where your family is? Do you know what's happened to them? My mother is in Paris—at least, I think she is. I haven't heard from her for such a long while."

Helen gulped.

"So, do you know where your mother is? Is she hiding? Is your father with her? Were they arrested?"

A warning bell was going off in Helen's mind. In the past couple of years, Maman had trained her and Henry to say little about who they were or where they had come from. *And definitely don't talk about being Jewish,* Maman had insisted. *The less you say, the better it will be for us.* Now this strange girl was peppering her with questions—personal questions. Could Helen trust her?

"Do you know where your family is?" Michelle persisted. And then she paused and sat back in her bed, eyeing Helen carefully. "We're all in the same boat, you know." She gestured around the room where other girls were getting dressed. "Everyone has parents who are hiding somewhere or were taken away somewhere. That girl over there"—she pointed toward a tall girl with red hair and freckles sprinkled across her nose—"her name is Anna. She actually saw her father get shot right in front of her. And that one over there"—she shifted and pointed toward a girl in the other corner—"she's Danielle. She went to two other countries with her parents before finally making it here." Michelle turned and looked back at Helen. "Do you want to know about me?"

Helen nodded.

"As I said, my mother is in Paris, hiding safely, I hope. I have no idea where my father is. He went to work one morning and never came home." Michelle waved her hand around the room again. "Your story probably isn't all that different from anyone else's in this room."

Helen glanced around at the other girls. Had everyone here been left behind by a mother or father? Had they all whispered quick good-byes not knowing when they would see their parents again? Helen responded hoarsely, "My mother brought us here— me and my brother. My father was arrested in Frankfurt. That's where we're from."

Michelle nodded. "You're lucky."

Lucky?

"At least you have a brother who's here with you. Most of us are alone."

Helen felt the blood rush to her cheeks.

"Let me tell you about the routine here," Michelle said, seeming to ignore Helen's distress. "Breakfast in the early morning and then classes. Lunch at noon and then chores. We have church services twice a day, morning and evening." She paused, noting the puzzled expression on Helen's face. "The nuns will explain all of that to you. There are performances sometimes," she continued. "The nuns think it's important to keep us entertained. A clown comes to do shows."

"You mean a circus clown?" Helen pictured some-one with a painted face and colorful costume.

Michelle frowned. "Not really. He does skits all by himself. And he pretends to be different characters.

You'll understand once you see him. Oh, and there are outings, to town. The department store isn't very big, but it's got the most wonderful dresses and ribbons and shoes. Sometimes the nuns will buy something special for you. And getting out of here, even for a morning, is the best!"

Just then, another series of bells rang, only louder and more insistent. Michelle jumped out of bed. "There's so much more I have to tell you." A cloud crossed her face. "Not all of it is as much fun as visits from the clown or even outings." She shook her head as if to clear those thoughts away. "But that's the breakfast bell. Get dressed as fast as you can and follow me. Most of the nuns are pretty nice here. But you have to watch out for Sister Agnes. She won't be happy if we're late."

Was that one of the nuns who had greeted her the previous night? The one who had sniffed the air and seemed to hate her? She had made the hairs on the back of Helen's neck stand straight up. Something inside of Helen told her she'd be better off staying away from that one.

"I think I may have met her already," Helen said.

Michelle pulled a face. "You can't forget Sister Agnes!"

The girls dressed hurriedly, and Helen followed Michelle down the long staircase to a huge dining hall, with at least ten large wooden tables lined up next to one another. Two old wrought-iron light fixtures were suspended from the wooden beams in the ceiling. Helen could see that this had once been a grand space. But the flowered wallpaper was peeling and torn, and the wooden floors were scratched and worn down in places. The room was already filled with girls and boys of all ages—at least sixty from what Helen could tell. They were standing behind their chairs, whispering and giggling to one another, and waiting for something—Helen didn't know what.

Michelle pointed to a chair next to hers and Helen stood behind it. She scanned the room, trying to find Henry in the crowd. But a moment later, a group of nuns entered and took their places behind a table at the front, and Helen shifted her attention to them. Sister Cecile was among them, smiling brightly and waving to all the children. Beside her was the nun who had scowled at her when she arrived, and her face this morning was still puckered and sour looking.

Michelle touched Helen's arm and, pointing to the mean-looking nun, whispered, "Sister Agnes."

The nun in charge, the tall one with the pointy nose who had done all the talking when Helen and Henry had arrived the night before, stood at the center of the table. She raised her hand and the room fell instantly silent. Then she closed her eyes, lowered her head, and began to recite a blessing of some kind. The children joined in to chant the responses. Finally, everyone in the room crossed themselves and in unison said, "Amen." The sound of chairs scraping across the wooden floor joined the chatter and laughter that resumed as the children finally took their seats.

Helen frowned. She had never heard this prayer before, and she certainly knew nothing about crossing herself! Of course, she knew what it was to be Catholic. There were many Catholic people who lived in Frankfurt. And Greta, the young Catholic girl who had often come to their house to help Maman with the cleaning, would cross herself whenever Helen asked how her mother was. Greta's mother had been sick for years, and when Helen would ask about her health, Greta would say, "I pray to God every day for her quick recovery." And then she'd reach up and touch her forehead, her stomach, and each shoulder in order, just as the children in the dining hall had done.

"It's all part of the routine here," Michelle said, seeing the confused look on Helen's face. "You'll get used to that as well."

"But aren't we all Jewish?" Helen whispered back.

Michelle laughed. "Of course!"

Helen sat back in her chair, her brain more muddled than ever.

"You'll find out everything you need to know soon enough," Michelle continued.

"But I don't understand."

Michelle sighed. "You will. I also had a lot of questions when I first got here. You have to be patient. And you need to eat something. You must be starving."

Several of the older boys and girls in the room were passing out plates of food. Helen suddenly realized how famished she was; she couldn't remember the last time she had had a proper meal. She gobbled up the cheese and fresh, crusty bread, slathered with butter and raspberry jam, and drank down the hot tea. This was not Maman's cooking, but it filled her stomach.

Finally, Helen glanced around the room again, once more searching for Henry. She spotted him on the other side, sitting at a table with other boys. But they were all talking to one another and paying no attention to the small boy who sat with his head down, playing with his food. It broke Helen's heart to see him all alone and still so sad. She rose from her table and was about to make her way to him when Sister Cecile suddenly appeared in front of her.

"Hello, Helen," the nun said. "How are you this morning?"

Helen glanced around Sister Cecile at Henry, who was still seated at the table, his head buried in his hands. She needed to get to him before breakfast was over. "I'm fine, thank you, Sister," she replied, hoping to move on.

"I have a message for you," Sister Cecile continued, her eyes following Helen's toward Henry. "You're wanted in the main office—you and your brother."

Helen thought about the tall nun with the long face who was in charge. "Have we done something wrong?"

Sister Cecile shook her head. "No, of course not. It's just a meeting to help you get settled. You must have a lot of questions about the convent."

That was certainly true. Helen nodded.

"All of those will be answered in this meeting." Then Sister Cecile leaned forward and lowered her voice. "It will take some time to adjust to being here. I understand that. Believe me, I do. And I want you to know that I'm here for you, if you need anything. Don't forget that."

Helen nodded again and finally went over to get Henry.

CHAPTER 4

Helen

The tall nun with the long face and dark eyes said that they must call her Mère Supérieure. She was the head of the convent and she sat behind a big wooden desk in her small office, staring over at Helen, who perched at the edge of a straight-backed chair, her hands folded in her lap. There was a framed painting of Jesus Christ hanging on the wall just behind the nun. The artist had painted a soft, glowing light around his head, and his penetrating blue eyes appeared to be staring straight at Helen.

"Are you finding your way around?" Mère Supérieure asked.

Helen glanced at Henry, who sat in the chair beside her, his head still hanging low on his chest. "Yes, I'm starting to," she replied.

"And did you sleep well last night? You must have been very tired."

At that, Helen hesitated. "I ... I had a hard time sleeping. I'm worried about my mother and father."

At the mention of their parents, Henry's head shot up. He looked at her and then at the nun. Helen could see the dark shadows that circled Henry's eyes. He probably hadn't slept well either, she thought.

Mère Supérieure sighed. "I don't have any news."

Helen swallowed hard. "I didn't think that you would. But I'm just wondering if there's any way that we can be in touch with our mother. Is that possible?" Her voice trailed off into a desperate plea.

Mère Supérieure shook her head. "Here is my advice to you both. It's best if you stop thinking about your parents for now. I don't expect I will hear anything for quite some time—if at all."

Stop thinking about Maman and Papa? That was unimaginable.

Mère Supérieure leaned forward in her chair. "I'm really not trying to be cruel." Her voice dropped when she said this and her eyes softened. "But there is so much for you to focus on while you are here. You must put your energy into understanding and following the rules of the convent. That's what is most important now."

Helen swallowed again and nodded. And then the nun began to talk about the convent, explaining that Jewish children from countries across Europe were all being protected here. And while the nuns were trying to maintain a safe place for these children, Mère Supérieure reminded Helen that southern France was still dangerous. The government of Marshal Philippe Pétain was in charge, and he was known to be a friend of Adolf Hitler. She said that there were Nazi soldiers moving through towns and villages in southern France, searching for Jews who might be hiding—children as well as grown-ups. "And those soldiers are also searching for anyone who may be hiding them," she added. "No one is entirely safe— not you and not us."

Helen's eyes widened as Mère Supérieure continued speaking. None of what she was saying was doing anything to help ease Helen's fears. "Excuse me," she interrupted. "But if it's so dangerous here, then wouldn't we have been better off just staying with our mother?" This place was beginning to feel as unsafe as Frankfurt or even Kronberg had been.

"No," Mère Supérieure replied. "Despite what I've said, you are safer here than you could possibly be anywhere else. But there are rules that you must follow, and follow them without hesitation. First, you must obey the sisters. They are here to protect you, and even if they seem harsh at times, please remember it is for your own good."

Helen thought about the nun who had sneered and sniffed the air—Sister Agnes. Mère Supérieure must be referring to her.

"Second, you must try to get along with the other children who are here. They will become your friends."

When Mère Supérieure said this, she stared straight at Henry, who turned away, avoiding her eyes. The nun stared a moment longer before turning back to Helen.

"Do not, and I repeat, do not, speak to anyone outside of the convent. We trust one another in here. But out there, we can never be sure. There are some in this town who know that we are hiding Jewish children here. And they believe in our mission. But it's difficult to know who might be a friend or not. Is that clear?"

Helen wasn't sure that she really understood what Mère Supérieure was saying. But after having run from Frankfurt, she understood that it was difficult to know who to trust. Helen nodded meekly and glanced again at the painting of Jesus. "I saw that all the children were reciting Catholic prayers this morning. I don't understand why."

Mère Supérieure's voice became even more serious. "That is perhaps the most important thing that I must explain to both of you," she said. "It's not that you will be hidden away while you are here, because in fact, everyone is living quite openly, as you can see. But the best way to keep you safe is to have you pretend to be Catholic children—orphans who have been sent to live here."

The pieces were beginning to fall into place for Helen.

"You will attend classes and go to church. We will teach you Catholic prayers and rituals. Learn these so well that you can practically do them in your sleep. That way, if you ever come in contact with anyone outside the convent walls, you will be able to pass yourself off as Catholic without hesitation."

Hiding but still visible, that's what they were all doing here, Helen realized. And pretending to be Catholic orphans was what would hopefully help keep them safe. But something still troubled her. "Our names—Helen and Henry Rosenthal. They don't exactly sound like Catholic names."

"Of course," the nun replied. "It will be necessary to change your names, make them sound less … Jewish. From now on, your last name will be Rochette."

Helen rolled the name around in her mouth, glancing once more at Henry, who dropped his head again. It would take some practice before she would be able to manage with this new last name. But she still had one more question, and thinking about it immediately filled her with some dread. "And what about our first names?" she stammered. "Will we have to change those as well?"

Mère Supérieure nodded. "I'm afraid so. Your new first names will be Claire and Andre."

"Claire Rochette." Helen whispered her new name out loud, trying to fit herself into it as if she were trying on a new dress or a new pair of shoes. How strange to think of herself as anyone but Helen Rosenthal.

"There is one last thing to complete the picture," said Mère Supérieure. "Your parents were killed in a fire. That's why you have come from Paris to live here. It's all part of your new identities."

Hearing the nun say the words *your parents were killed in a fire* sent shivers down Helen's spine, even though she knew it wasn't true. Beside her, Henry's face went completely white. She reached out and placed her hand on top of his arm, squeezing tightly. Henry didn't move and he didn't push her away.

"I know this is a lot of information to take in," Mère Supérieure continued. "Practice your new names. Remember your new identities. There can be no mistakes here," she added. "The safety of every child in this convent—the safety of us all—depends on each one of us."

With that, she stood as if to dismiss them. Helen rose as well, pulling Henry up with her. Then the head nun stopped her.

"Claire, I'd like you to stay behind a moment. Andre, you may go."

Helen found it disturbing to hear Mère Supérieure address them by their new names. Beside her, she could feel Henry stiffen before he finally turned and shuffled from the room. Mère Supérieure waited for the door to close before beginning to speak again.

"I'm concerned about your brother—his silence."

Helen gulped. She was worried about that, too. "He's not himself, ma'am ... um ... Mère Supérieure. But I'm sure he'll be fine." Of course, she wasn't sure about that, but she couldn't let the head nun know.

"It's just that he must fit in like everyone else."

Helen frowned. If Henry didn't *fit in*, then what? "He's scared, Mère Supérieure. We both are," she added, her voice dropping.

"I understand," Mère Supérieure replied. "But he must learn to adjust or we will have to ... we will have to rethink your situation."

Helen didn't like where Mère Supérieure was going with this. If Henry didn't *adjust*, if he didn't start to talk, then would the two of them be sent away? Or just Henry? And to where? Germany, where they had come from, was completely unsafe. And Maman had said there was no other place here in southern France. Even Mère Supérieure had told her that Nazi soldiers were roaming the towns and villages looking for Jews. Helen knew that she had to take care of Henry; Maman had told her that. But this responsibility was feeling bigger by the minute.

"Please, Mère Supérieure," Helen said, glancing once more at the portrait of Jesus. "I'm sure my brother isn't the first boy who's had trouble settling in." It was bold of her to confront Mère Supérieure like this. But what other choice did she have? She had to stand up for Henry. "Everything is so different here—for all of us. And he's so young."

Didn't this head nun understand how hard it was for them to have been uprooted and brought to this strange place? Even Helen was shaking on the inside, even though she might have appeared calm on the outside. *And I'm fourteen*, she thought. Helen understood that Henry's silence looked like defiance. But behind the clenched fists, and glares, she knew he was simply scared.

"Henry's not trying to be difficult, Mère Supérieure," she added. "He just needs time."

Mère Supérieure sighed deeply. "It's Andre," she said. "Please remember that." And then she waved her hand, signaling that Helen was free to go. But not before adding, "Not too much time."

CHAPTER 5

Henry

Henry sat in a small classroom with other children his age. At the front of the room, one of the nuns— the nice one, Sister Cecile—was teaching something that she called catechism, a bunch of questions and answers that the children had to memorize.

"What is the chief purpose of all people?" Sister Cecile asked.

"To glorify God and enjoy him forever," the students replied all together.

Henry wasn't paying attention. Instead, he was hunched over a small notebook, gripping a pencil. Sister Cecile had given him the notebook, saying that maybe if he didn't want to talk, he could use it as a diary and write down his thoughts and feelings.

Henry didn't like the idea of having a diary. *Diaries are for girls*, he thought. Helen had owned a diary back in Frankfurt. She had practically exploded with anger the day Henry snuck into her room and got his hands on it. He just wanted to peek inside. But Maman and Papa had been more cross with him than they had ever been before, telling him he was not allowed to go into Helen's room without her permission—EVER! Helen's diary hadn't even been that interesting as far as Henry was concerned, just a bunch of boring notes about sunsets and food, and dresses that she wanted to wear. No, he didn't like the idea of having a diary. His would be a code book, for important ideas and secret thoughts that no one else could see.

Henry stared down at the white page. And then he lowered his pencil and wrote, *My name is ...* He paused, staring at the blankness that followed. Finally, in large block letters, he wrote HENRY ROSENTHAL. He paused again, hovering his pencil above the page for a moment before lowering it to carefully draw a small Star of David—first a right-side-up triangle and then an upside-down triangle over it. There had been a big star just like this one hanging over the door of their synagogue back in Frankfurt. It had been destroyed the night Papa was taken. Finally, Henry sat back in his chair, examining his work. Henry Rosenthal was his name, not that new one the tall nun with the pointy nose and bushy eyebrows had given him—*Andre*. She had told him that he had to change his name just the way Maman used to tell him to change his socks. But how could he do that? It was like asking him to take someone else's head and stick it on his body. That would be impossible!

Maman had often told him that he had been named after her father, whom Henry had never known. His name had been Aharon. She had said that it was an honor to carry her late father's name. What would his grandfather Aharon have thought if he knew that Henry was being forced to give it up now? Where was the honor in that? Besides, he knew that the name Henry meant "ruler of the home." Papa had always joked that Henry was the real head of the household. "You rule the roost, my little Henry," Papa had always said. Henry didn't know what the name Andre meant, but it probably wasn't as special as ruler of the household.

Sometimes, Papa had called him by the nickname Henny, which Henry had to admit he didn't always like. He was afraid that someone might shorten that to Hen and make fun of him—maybe by walking around clucking like a chicken. He would have pounded anyone who had tried that. But a nickname was different than changing your name altogether. A nickname was something someone gave you because they loved you—like Papa did. *DOES*, he corrected himself. He had to keep hoping that Papa was somewhere safe, thinking about Henry as much as Henry was thinking about him.

He bent over his page again and wrote the word *safe*. The nun with the pointy nose had said that this convent was going to be a safe place for Henry as long as he followed the rules. She said that many children were being harbored here. The word *harbored* was a new one for him. He knew that boats could sit in a harbor, where they were protected from the sea. But he hadn't thought about that when it came to people.

The lesson was continuing at the front of the classroom.

"What do the scriptures principally teach?" Sister Cecile was asking.

"What we are to believe concerning God, and what duty God requires of us," the children droned.

It had been more than a week since Henry had arrived here with his sister. *No*, he corrected himself, when he had been *left* here with Helen. *Arrived* made it sound as if they had come for a vacation—

like the time he and his family had gone to the Baltic Sea for a holiday. Being here was nothing like being on vacation. In the time since Henry had been *left* here, he had pretty much kept to himself. The other boys in his room seemed friendly enough, but Henry couldn't bring himself to talk to them, or to anyone, for that matter. He hadn't even said a word to Helen, though she begged him every day to say something— anything! She even told him that if he didn't start to talk, they might not be able to stay at the convent. That was fine as far as Henry was concerned. Maybe then, Maman would have to come and pick them up. He knew in his heart that that probably wouldn't happen. But just the same, it felt better to stay quiet. Keeping everything inside was better than letting it all out. Maybe he was *harboring* his feelings inside of him, protecting them, the way the children were being protected here. He would talk again when the time was right.

Henry bent over his page once more and wrote the word *harbor.*

There were so many new routines to follow at this place: getting up at dawn when the bells rang, eating meals in the grand dining hall, going to classes, always staying together as a group, always listening to the nuns when they spoke to you. One of the things he didn't mind was going to church services. The chapel was a quiet place where no one asked you to talk or explain yourself. He didn't even mind crossing himself, although at first, that had seemed so strange. But he had quickly learned to take his right hand and touch it first to his forehead, then his stomach, then each of his shoulders. Once, he had made the mistake of touching his stomach before his forehead. The head nun with the pointy nose had corrected him. "Don't make that mistake again," she had said. "No one else sees you here in the convent. But if that were to happen out there"—she pointed somewhere beyond the chapel windows—"someone might guess that you don't belong here."

Henry picked up his pencil and once more wrote his name, Henry Rosenthal, this time in bigger, bolder letters.

The thing that Henry liked most about church was talking to God—not talking out loud, but talking to God in his head and in his heart. It didn't matter that he was a young Jewish boy sitting in this Catholic chapel with that gigantic statue of Jesus Christ towering like a mountain on top of the pulpit. It was quiet in this church, and peaceful. He prayed for Maman to come back for him as quickly as possible. He prayed that Papa would be safe and would come home soon. He prayed that they would all go back to their house in Frankfurt and everything would go back to normal, the normal that he had known before all those laws and rules had been passed against Jewish people. He even prayed that Helen would stop treating him like a baby. He believed that God heard him even if he didn't say a word.

Henry stared back at the page in front of him. Finally, in very small letters, he wrote the name Andre Rochette. He sat back and stared at the strange new name, outlining the letters with one finger. Then, he quickly crossed them out with thick black strokes. He sighed, a deep, long exhale of his breath. And then finally, he wrote the new name again.

CHAPTER 6

Helen

Sister Agnes was reading a story to the class. "The Ant and the Grasshopper" was about an ant that diligently collected food to store for the approaching winter. A playful grasshopper mocked the ant, telling him that he should forget his work and come play instead. But the ant refused, warning the grasshopper that it would be sorry when winter was upon them and the grasshopper had nothing to eat. Sure enough, when winter arrived, the grasshopper came to the ant begging for food, but the ant would not help him.

The story was childish, and well below the level of reading that Helen had done back in Frankfurt. At home, she had devoured complex books about history and science and other countries in the world. Still, she wouldn't have minded hearing such an easy story, were it not for the fact that Sister Agnes was such a slow and tedious reader. Helen marveled at how anyone could take a simple tale like this one and turn it into such an agonizing experience!

She stifled a yawn and glanced over at Michelle, who sat at the desk next to her. Just the day before, Michelle had gone on one of those special outings to town and had returned with the most beautiful deep green ribbon, which she wore today, wrapped around her ponytail and tied in a big bow. Helen gazed longingly at the ribbon, wondering when she, too, would have a chance to go to town—to walk out the doors of the convent, even if only for a few hours. None of the nuns had offered her that chance yet. As Helen stared at the ribbon, Michelle leaned her head onto one arm, her eyes fluttered shut, and her mouth went slack. She was asleep! If Sister Agnes caught her, she would have a fit. Helen shifted in her chair and cleared her throat, hoping Michelle might hear her and wake up. No such luck! Helen wanted to reach across the aisle and nudge her friend but she was afraid the movement would draw Sister Agnes's attention to the two of them. And that would be no help at all.

Over the last few weeks, Helen's instincts about Sister Agnes had proved to be correct. She was indeed the nun to be feared at the convent. She sneered at everyone. She doled out punishments before you had even realized what crime you had committed. Everyone was afraid of her, but Helen most of all. It appeared that Sister Agnes was making Helen her special project, singling her out for the slightest infraction of the rules. Helen tried to steer clear of this nun. But that was proving difficult.

"And so, the lessons that we learn from this fable are the following," Sister Agnes droned from the front of the room. "It is always best to be prepared. And one must have compassion for others in times of need."

Compassion! Helen almost laughed out loud. *What about having some compassion for us?* Just the day before, Sister Agnes had stopped her in the hallway to tell her that her skirt was wrinkled. It was true that she had forgotten to hang it up the night before. But what was she supposed to do with a wrinkled skirt? She had smoothed it down as much as possible, but that obviously wasn't enough for Sister Agnes. As punishment, she had made Helen wash all the dinner dishes. And for what? A skirt with a few creases in it! It had been nearly midnight before Helen had finally fallen into bed.

"Open your notebooks and write the words *compassion* and *charity*," continued Sister Agnes. "And then list ten ways in which you will practice these virtues."

The door to the classroom suddenly opened and an older girl came in. She walked up to Sister Agnes and whispered something in her ear.

"I must go and attend to some matters in Mère Supérieure's office," Sister Agnes said. "I expect you all to work in silence until I return."

Once she had left the classroom, the students released a big collective sigh, and they all began to whisper.

"She makes me so nervous," Helen said, turning to Michelle, who was now awake, stretching and yawning beside her.

"She makes everyone nervous."

"But I feel as if she has it in for me in particular." Helen reminded Michelle about the incident with her wrinkled skirt. "And that's just one example."

Michelle looked sympathetic. "You can't take it personally. She likes to pick on the new ones—teach them a lesson. It's sort of like your initiation into this place."

"But how long will it last?" Helen wasn't sure how much more of this she could take.

"Usually until someone else arrives."

At that, Helen groaned.

"She's coming!" The boy posted as lookout at the classroom door relayed the message to the class. The chatter came to an abrupt stop as everyone grabbed their pens and bent over their notebooks, scribbling furiously. Helen looked down at the words, *compassion* and *charity*. She thought for a moment and then wrote, *I will try to have more patience with Henry.*

Her brother had still not spoken a word, though several weeks had passed since their arrival here. She continued to believe that he would end his silence soon, just as he had in the past. Still, she was trying to avoid Mère Supérieure these days, afraid that the head nun would announce that Henry had not fit in after all and was going to be sent away. *Oh, if only Maman were here*, thought Helen for the millionth time. Not that her mother could ever persuade Henry out of his silence either. No one could. But at least Maman could comfort him—and her. But there had still been no word from her mother.

Sister Agnes reentered the classroom and began to walk up and down the aisles, stopping now and then to look at a student's notebook. Helen stiffened as the nun approached her desk and paused. She bent forward to read over Helen's shoulder and then straightened.

"You have only written one line," she began. She sniffled and took a tissue from her pocket, dabbing her nose. "And what, may I ask, have you been doing in all the time I was out of the classroom?"

"I-I was … I was thinking, Sister Agnes," Helen stammered.

"Less thinking and more action would do you well," the nun replied.

Helen lowered her head. "Yes, Sister Agnes." She hoped that was it. She prayed that the nun would continue her walk around the classroom and leave her alone. But that was not to be.

"Please stand," Sister Agnes commanded.

Helen squeezed her eyes shut, took a deep breath, and slid out from behind her desk. She glanced over at Michelle, who gave her a compassionate nod. Sister Agnes was staring at Helen, examining her from head to toe like an army general inspecting a troop member. Finally, her eyes came to rest on Helen's shoes.

"They're filthy, full of dust," Sister Agnes said, scrunching her nose and sneering.

"I'm sorry, Sister Agnes," Helen whispered. "The yard was muddy this morning. I was going to clean them later, when I had a chance …" Her voice trailed off and she stood meekly, head bowed.

"Excuses are not good enough." Sister Agnes folded her arms across her chest. "As punishment, you will mop all the floors in the upstairs hallway today. Strong hands make for a strong mind. You may sit."

With that, Sister Agnes continued her walk around the classroom. Helen sank into her seat. Several other girls looked away. Michelle gazed sympathetically as Helen pressed her hands up to her eyes, willing herself not to cry. She refused to show any weakness before this nun, no matter how difficult she was making her life. Michelle said that all this would stop when someone new arrived. That couldn't happen soon enough.

CHAPTER 7

Helen

Several days later, just as Helen was about to head into the dining hall, Sister Agnes stopped her in the hallway.

Helen's heart froze. *What now*, she wondered. She had done all the mopping that the nun had ordered her to do. On top of that, her skirt and blouse were neat and wrinkle free, her bed had been made with military precision, her shoes were shiny, and all her homework had been completed and handed in on time. With what could the sister possibly find fault? Helen kept her stare even as Sister Agnes looked her up and down. Luckily, the nun seemed to approve of her appearance.

"I would like you and your brother to meet me at the front doors immediately after breakfast," Sister Agnes began.

Helen exhaled the breath she had been holding. *No punishment!* But then she froze again. Perhaps this had something to do with Henry and his ongoing silence. Maybe a decision had been made to send her and her brother away. But Sister Agnes's next words were more startling than ever.

"We will go shopping in town. I had hoped your brother would begin to talk before taking him out of the convent." She sniffed a bit when she said that part. "But his silence may be beneficial for this kind of outing. Besides, I know that you are both in need of some personal clothing items."

Helen's mouth gaped open. "Um ... yes ... of course, Sister Agnes."

The nun sniffed. "That is all. Don't be late." And with that, she turned and marched away.

"Thank you!" Helen called out to her quickly receding form. An outing to town! Helen had all but given up hope of being one of the lucky ones who got to leave the convent—to step outside the walls of this place that was a refuge but felt at times like a prison. This was the reward she had been waiting for. She rushed through breakfast, then grabbed Henry and arrived at the convent doors just as Sister Agnes was coming down the stairs.

The nun scowled at them both. "Walk behind me," she instructed. "Do not say a word to anyone." With that, she opened the doors and walked out. Helen and Henry followed close on her heels.

Helen breathed in deeply as they wound their way along the dusty road that led to town. Was it her imagination, or did the air smell different beyond the convent gates? It was somehow fresher and cleaner, and the sky looked so much bigger and bluer. A full-winged bird flew in sluggish circles high above her head, and bees hovered in clusters by the side of the road. The sun was playing hide-and-seek between the trees that towered on either side of them. There were moments when they walked in cool, deep shadows, and then, suddenly, the sun exploded in full force, wrapping them in its warmth. Helen let her head fall back and felt the mid-morning rays pour across her face.

It was true that they were in desperate need of some clothing. They had left Kronberg so quickly on that fateful night, and they hadn't brought many things with them—just a small suitcase each. She had only a few skirts and blouses and had worn them so many times that her cuffs and hems were frayed and thinning. Sister Agnes had told her she could get one new blouse and skirt, and for Henry, a couple of pairs of trousers and a pair of shoes. Although her brother hadn't said a word to her about needing new shoes, she could see that his had become so tight he could barely lace them. And she guessed that his toes must be pinched, because he limped along beside her, struggling to keep up with Sister Agnes striding up ahead. Every once in a while, she turned back to bark at them. "Stop dawdling and walk quicker." Helen wanted to walk as slowly as she possibly could—didn't want this part of the outing to end. But with a deep sigh, she grabbed Henry by the arm and dragged him forward. And then, they turned a corner and the town came into view.

Helen felt her breath immediately quicken and her chest constrict. A banner with the emblem of the Nazi army—the swastika—was draped down the length of a building. It rippled in lazy waves as a small breeze passed over it. Helen had an instant and terrifying memory of the night Papa had been taken. These same flags of red and black had adorned all the main buildings in her city. The pleasure of the walk from the convent to town was instantly forgotten. Helen felt Henry stiffen next to her. His eyes grew round with fear and he stopped in his tracks. She paused beside him and placed a reassuring arm on his shoulder.

"It's okay, Henry. Just stay close to me and we'll be fine." Her words sounded more confident than she felt.

She had an overwhelming need to protect him. Should she hold his hand? He probably wouldn't like that. He might even get angry at her. At another time, he might have shouted at her not to treat him like a baby. But Helen hadn't heard the sound of Henry's voice in so long. And now was not the time to risk drawing attention to themselves. She dropped her arm by her side and continued to walk after Sister Agnes. After another moment's hesitation, Henry followed. They continued walking, heads down, eyes on the ground, until they finally reached the small clothing store at the far end of the road.

"Once we're inside, I'll give you exactly a half an hour to gather the things you need," Sister Agnes said, pausing outside. "There is a clock on the wall of the store, so please watch it carefully. I also need some things for the convent, so I will meet up with you at the front door," the nun added. Sister Agnes didn't appear to be terribly bothered by the banner with the swastika on it. Perhaps she had seen it before on her many walks to town.

"Remember to stay together and speak to no one," the nun added.

"Stay with me when we get inside, Henry," Helen said. "I'm going to get my things first and then I'll help you with yours."

Henry frowned. She knew he didn't want her hovering over him. And he probably didn't want to stand around watching her go through girly clothing. But like it or not, there was no way she was going to let him loose in the shop. They needed to stay together.

"Well?" she asked.

Reluctantly, he nodded his head. Sister Agnes opened the door to allow the children to enter the store.

Helen gasped when she walked inside. Michelle was right. The department store was wonderful. The racks were filled with such lovely dresses and blouses the likes of which she had not seen in such a long time. A young girl walked past her, holding on to a woman's hand. The girl wore a pale blue dress with a matching ribbon tied around her head. It reminded Helen of Michelle's green ribbon. Helen felt a sudden pang in her heart. She and Maman had shopped in stores bigger than this one, spending hours digging through carousels of clothing until they found the perfect dress for a special occasion or the perfect gift for a friend's birthday party. Those days seemed impossibly far away.

When Helen looked around, she realized that Sister Agnes had disappeared—probably to go and fetch the things for the convent. But Henry, too, seemed to have vanished. Why hadn't he listened to her? she wondered with a stab of irritation. She wasn't trying to boss him around; she was just trying to look out for him. That's what an older sister did!

She looked around again. The store seemed safe enough. There were lots of other shoppers, mostly women and children, walking up and down the aisles. No one was paying attention to her. She would quickly find the things she needed and then go and search for Henry. With any luck, he would have found shoes on his own. That would probably make him feel good, she thought, being able to find the things he needed without her help.

Helen turned back to the shelves. In addition to the blouse and skirt, she also needed some underwear and stockings. She was sure that Sister Agnes would understand that those were necessary. And then there was a ribbon. She hoped she might find something like that. She found her personal items quickly and gathered them together in her arms. She even found a small hair clip. It wasn't a ribbon like Michelle's, but she knew it would be perfect for her short curls. She hoped that Sister Agnes would agree to let her have it. *Now, where's Henry?* she wondered again. She began to walk over to the shoe section of the store, sighing longingly as she passed the pretty dresses once more.

She saw the soldiers as soon as she turned a corner.

CHAPTER 8

Helen

Three Nazi soldiers stood with their backs to Helen, blocking her way. She stopped in the middle of the aisle. Her heart began to race and she felt the hairs at the back of her neck stand straight up. She breathed in quick and shallow gulps, trying to get some air and calm herself. And then, slowly but surely, she began to back up, placing one foot behind the other, trying to creep away from the soldiers who were still turned away from her. If they didn't see her, then everything would be fine, she told herself. Three more steps, and then two, and in another moment, she would be safe.

That was when Helen noticed that the soldiers were bent forward, stooped over as if they were talking to someone much smaller than they were. A cold pain gripped at her heart. There was only one person they might be speaking to. She inched forward and peered more closely. And sure enough, there was Henry, standing in front of the soldiers.

Her heart began to beat at a full gallop. Henry's face was drained of color, as white as Maman's had been the night she had left them at the convent. He clenched and unclenched his fists. His eyes bulged as they darted from soldier to soldier. His whole body was shaking.

The soldiers seemed to be in an animated conversation with him, though she could see that Henry had not opened his mouth. At first, Helen couldn't hear anything that the soldiers were saying. The blood had rushed to her head and was pounding so loud that it blocked out any other sound. She dropped the items of clothing that she was carrying along with the hair clip. And with all the courage she could muster, she approached the group. Her legs were shaking so badly she thought she might fall down before she even reached them.

"Excuse me," she began as she entered the circle of soldiers and felt herself being swallowed up. She willed herself not to stare at them. Instead, she looked straight at Henry.

"There you are," she said, trying to keep her voice as even as possible. "I've been searching everywhere for you. It's time to go. Come with me right now."

Henry's eyes continued to dart everywhere. He opened his mouth and then closed it shut. Helen was just about to take him by the arm and pull him along when one of the soldiers put his hand out to stop her.

"He is with you?" He was speaking in French, but with a terrible accent, the kind that Papa had when he'd tried to practice the few words of French that he knew. She and Henry had laughed at their father then. There was nothing funny about this situation.

Helen nodded at the soldier. "My brother."

He bent his face close to Henry's. His uniform was brown, the jacket held together with a thick black belt and shiny buckle. And he wore an armband with the same Nazi insignia that she had seen on the flag draped down the building in the central square. The red and black patch seemed to glow. She looked away, still trying to catch her breath.

"We wondered what he was doing here alone," the soldier said. "But when we asked, he wouldn't answer us."

That's when Helen looked up into the soldier's face.

"He's very shy—barely says a word, even to me." She tried to smile as she said this, hoping her lips didn't tremble too much.

The soldier straightened and nodded. "Ah, shy. I understand," he said. "I have a young son who is also shy." Then he bent to Henry once more. "No need to be afraid, young man. What's your name?"

Henry shrank even farther away from the soldier. Helen noticed that one or two customers passing by were slowing in curiosity. But she realized that most of the shoppers had disappeared from sight. They were giving Helen and Henry a wide berth, not wanting to be anywhere near Nazi soldiers who might be asking questions.

"Won't you tell me your name?" the soldier asked again.

Henry was breathing loudly in and out through his nose, and his lips were trembling. Helen knew that she needed to jump in. With her stomach churning, she stepped in front of Henry, opened her mouth, and began, "His name is He—"

Just then, she felt a strong tug on her arm. She stopped and looked back at Henry, who was squeezing her with a force she didn't know he possessed. The fear was still there in his eyes. But there was also something else—a warning. Helen knew instantly what he was trying to tell her. She closed her eyes, trying to steady herself. Then she opened them, took a deep breath, and began to speak again.

"His name is Andre," she said. "Andre Rochette. And I'm Claire." She curtsied to the soldiers. "We really must go," she said. She took Henry's arm again and was about to walk out of the circle of soldiers with him when the soldier stepped in front of her.

"Where do the two of you live?" he asked. "Perhaps we could take you back to your home."

"Thank you," Helen replied. "But we live at the convent—very close by. We're here with one of the sisters." Where, oh where, was Sister Agnes? Helen stood on her toes to scan the store.

The soldier nodded understandingly. "And your parents?"

Helen bit her bottom lip. "Gone," she replied. "A-a fire. My brother and I were the only ones pulled out alive." She reached up and crossed herself after she said this, and then folded her hands together and bowed her head.

Was there enough emotion in her voice? Did she appear sad and mournful?

"Of course," the soldier said quickly. "My sympathies."

That was the exact moment that Sister Agnes appeared, rounding an aisle and barging up to Helen,

Henry, and the trio of soldiers. Her face went pale as she sized up the situation.

"Claire. Andre. I've been searching the store for you," she exclaimed.

The soldier snapped his heels together and bowed crisply. Then he took his cap off his head and placed it underneath his arm. "Not to worry, Sister," he said. "We've been having a lovely chat with these two."

Sister Agnes looked as if she was about to pass out. Her mouth hung open and her face began to twitch.

"We offered them a ride home, but the young girl explained that they live at the convent. Poor orphans," he added in a compassionate whisper.

"Yes, well, thank you," Sister Agnes stammered. "Come, children. We must leave. Now!" she added, as she turned to go.

Helen took Henry by the arm and was just about to follow when the soldier stopped her once more, this time with a hand on her shoulder.

"Be careful when you are out on your own," he said. "There are some disgusting people passing through who may try to take advantage of you—or your shy younger brother." Then he leaned forward once more and lowered his voice. "The Jews are every-where, you know."

Helen felt a shiver go down her spine and she shuddered. She could smell fish and stale cigarettes on his breath. She tried not to flinch. When she glanced at Henry again, she could see that his eyes had widened once more. She willed herself to smile at the soldier and curtsied again.

The soldier led them to the door. On the way out, Helen passed the young girl in the blue dress and matching ribbon she had seen earlier. The girl was standing hand in hand with her mother. Suddenly, the girl raised her arm straight in front of her in a Nazi salute. The soldier paused and then clicked his heels together and saluted back to her. Helen winced, and the blood drained from her face once more as she made eye contact with the young girl who stood with her arm outstretched.

Helen tightened her grip on Henry and followed Sister Agnes out the door.

CHAPTER 9

Henry

No one talked on the walk back to the convent. Helen shuffled along the road with her head down and that look on her face as if she'd seen a ghost. Sister Agnes was practically running ahead of them. And Henry was dragging his hurting feet, knowing he had to keep up with his sister and that mean nun who always yelled. The whole scene in the store played through his mind like the worst nightmare, the kind he'd had when he was just a little boy. Sometimes he didn't even know what had woken him in the middle of the night screaming. Maman would be the one to rush in and calm him down. Well, today, he was clear about what had caused the nightmare, though he wasn't sure what part had been worse—the Nazi soldier talking to him, or that girl with her arm up in the air in that ugly salute.

They were the same kinds of soldiers who had taken Papa. Henry knew that. That's what had made him so scared when they walked up to him in the first place. The one who had asked all the questions had bad breath, like he'd been eating the fish that the cook at the convent had prepared the other night. It had made Henry want to throw up. He had wanted to yell at the soldiers. He had wanted to jump at them and hit them and make them tell him where they had taken his father. But the sight of the soldiers had also scared him even more than having Maman leave him at the convent. He couldn't move, and he couldn't make himself speak. And then Helen had walked up, looking as scared as he felt. And now, the mean nun was probably going to punish both of them for dis-obeying her and talking with the soldiers in the first place. Not that they could have done anything about that. The soldiers had come up to *him*. He had just been minding his own business in the store, looking for new shoes so that he could stop wearing the ones he had on—the ones that squeezed his toes so badly, he couldn't walk without limping. But the soldiers had appeared so fast, he hadn't even had time to find the shoes. And now, he'd probably never get them.

Helen suddenly ran ahead to catch up with Sister Agnes. Henry struggled to keep up and get close enough to hear what his sister was saying. She was talking fast, as if she didn't want the nun to interrupt her. And her hands were flying all around her head.

"I was watching him, Sister. I promise I was. And then I lost track of him. It was only for a minute. I didn't think anything bad would happen in a minute. I figured he'd be fine and we'd get the things we needed and leave. But the soldiers just appeared out of nowhere."

The nun stopped and whirled to face Helen. "Do you know how dangerous that was? Do you realize what could have happened?"

"I know, Sister Agnes. But this wasn't our fault."

"I told you to speak with no one!"

"But you never told us that there might be Nazi soldiers in the store."

Sister Agnes looked madder than Henry had ever seen. There was practically fire coming out of her eyes. But there was also something different about the look on her face. She looked scared. That was something Henry hadn't seen before.

"I ... thought I might lose you today," Sister Agnes said, her face pale and her voice shaking. "Those soldiers are searching for Jews. And not just grown-ups.

They are searching for children, like the two of you."
She swept her arm out to include Henry.

Sister Agnes sounded as if she was really worried
about them. And Helen looked as if she might cry.
He wanted to do something to help, but he felt more
helpless than ever.

"It was a mistake to leave the convent," Sister
Agnes continued. The worried look disappeared. "I'm
afraid that will have to be the only time for you two—
and the last time for all of you!"

Then she turned and kept marching down the
road. Helen dropped back to walk with Henry. At
first, she didn't say a word. He looked up at her. He
hadn't wanted to make her mad, and he hated it when
he saw that she was scared. He wanted to tell her
that he felt that way, too, and that they were in this
together. He wanted to tell her that he would always
try to watch out for her. She had spoken up for him
in the store, but he was the one who had stopped her
from saying his real name. They could have been
in even bigger trouble if she'd done that. He'd even
looked sad and had made his lower lip shake when
Helen had talked about their parents being dead. Did
she realize what he had done? Did she understand
that he was looking out for her, too? He wanted to tell
her all of those things. But no words came out of his
mouth.

They walked together a little while longer until Helen finally turned to him. "I know what you were trying to do in there, Henry," she said. "I almost said your name. If you hadn't grabbed my arm and stopped me, I don't know what would have happened."

So, she does understand after all.

"That was pretty brave of you."

He glanced up at her and the slightest smile crept across his face.

Helen sighed and looked up ahead to where Sister Agnes was still marching along, her arms swinging furiously back and forth with every long step that she took. "I don't know what's going to happen when we get back to the convent. We're probably going to be in real trouble, that's for sure. But I want to thank you for stopping me in there."

Henry felt his heart swell. *She knows!* She understood what he had done. That was most important.

"Sometimes I think I need to protect you," Helen continued. "But I'm glad you're here to protect me, too."

Together, they continued walking toward the convent. Henry still felt afraid and still felt as if he wasn't ready to speak. But something had changed for him. Helen had called him brave. He needed to believe it was true.

CHAPTER 10

Helen

As soon as they arrived back at the convent, Sister Agnes stormed ahead to the head nun's office. And not long after that, Mère Supérieure summoned them to meet with her. Helen wasn't surprised, but she dreaded what was to come. What had Sister Agnes meant when she'd said it was the last time they would be able to leave the convent? And would they be sent away from here? If that happened, then how would Maman ever find them? How would she ever come back for them? How would they ever be a whole family again? Those thoughts were more terrifying than anything else.

"We didn't do anything wrong," Helen cried once they were seated in front of Mère Supérieure.

"Didn't do anything wrong?" the head nun asked. "There are so many things that you did wrong— leaving your brother alone, talking to those soldiers. How can you not see that?"

Helen did not back down. She clenched her fists in her lap and sat farther up in the chair. "Sister Agnes told us we could get our things on our own. And we didn't see the soldiers. They just appeared out of nowhere."

Mère Supérieure barely heard what she was saying. "You knew you were not supposed to talk to anyone when you were out. Don't you realize what danger you might have put this convent in? The other children?"

"But the soldiers questioned us!" Helen persisted. "Were we supposed to turn and walk away? Don't you think that would have been even more dangerous?" How could the head nun not understand this?

Mère Supérieure sighed.

"We didn't give anything away," Helen continued. "We remembered our names—Claire and Andre." She reached over and squeezed Henry's hand as she carefully sidestepped around the part where she had very nearly blurted their real names.

Henry looked at her as she spoke. There was a mixture of understanding and pride on his face. Then he turned and stared defiantly at Mère Supérieure.

The nun shook her head. "Thank goodness you remembered what you had been taught. And we can only hope that it was enough. But how can I make you understand the risk that you took?" The head nun's voice was sounding more tired and less cross.

"I'm sorry, Mère Supérieure. And I know how angry Sister Agnes is. I'm sure there will be some punishment for us." Helen hung her head and waited. She would take whatever Sister Agnes doled out: washing dishes for a month, scrubbing floors, making everyone's beds—whatever it was, she could handle it. *Just don't send us away,* Helen prayed.

"Sister Agnes was terrified!" Mère Supérieure said. "She worries about you and all of the children at the convent. And it's not about being punished. It's just that ..." She paused and Helen looked up.

"It's the first time that the Nazis have appeared in our town," the head nun said. "We've seen their flags and we know they're in this area. But we've never spotted them this close to our convent before."

This admission was huge, Helen realized. And terrifying. The danger that the head nun had alluded to—soldiers searching for Jews in surrounding towns and villages—was getting closer. Hitler's soldiers were nearby. This place of safety was feeling less and less secure.

"But if you didn't know about the Nazis, and Sister Agnes didn't know about them, how could my brother and I have known they would be in the store?"

"Yes, I suppose you're right." Mère Supérieure sighed again and shook her head. "I don't know what to think. The Nazis being this close changes everything for us."

It felt for a moment as if Mère Supérieure had forgotten that Helen and her brother were in her office. She stared off into space, her lips moving as if she was still talking but no sound was coming out. Finally, her gaze came back to rest on the children. "I must discuss this with the other sisters." She paused and then added, "That's all. You may both go."

Helen stood, grabbed Henry by the arm, and the two of them fled the room.

Henry bolted down the hall and up the staircase before Helen had a chance to talk to him. But Michelle was waiting for her outside the head nun's office.

"I heard what happened when you went into town. Everyone's talking about it. Are you okay?" Michelle took Helen's arm and steered her down the hallway to a quiet classroom where the nuns would not hear their conversation. Her eyes were filled with concern.

Helen quickly told her about their encounter with the Nazi soldiers. "It was terrible. They were this close to us." She held her hands inches apart. "And they started asking questions about who we were and where we were living, and where our parents were. I was shaking so hard I thought I'd fall down." Even now, her stomach was churning just recalling the events in the store.

Michelle gasped. "I've been to town with the sisters a few times. I've seen those flags on the buildings. But I've never seen any soldiers."

Helen nodded. "That's what Mère Supérieure said. They've never been this close to the convent. What do you think it means?"

Michelle shook her head. "I don't know."

The girls stood in silence and then Michelle spoke again. "Maybe it was only a one-time thing. Maybe the soldiers were just passing through town and now they're gone."

Helen looked doubtful. "Mère Supérieure was pretty upset about the whole thing."

"But we have to keep believing that we're safe here, right?" Michelle paused. "Mère Supérieure said we're still safe, didn't she?"

"She just said that she needs time to think."

"Think about what?"

Helen shrugged her shoulders. She had no answer.

"Do you think you're going to be in trouble with Sister Agnes?" Michelle finally asked.

"I have no idea. I still say that Henry and I did nothing wrong. But there's no telling what Sister Agnes will twist this into."

A punishment from the mean nun seemed almost insignificant right now—and the least of her worries. She could deal with whatever the nuns doled out to her. What she couldn't shake was the feeling that the danger out there everyone spoke of was getting closer and closer to her and everyone at the convent. She looked over at Michelle. Her friend hadn't stood inches from the Nazis like she had. Michelle hadn't felt the soldier's breath on her face or heard him say that the Jews are disgusting. Like Michelle, Helen wanted to believe that things wouldn't get any worse and the only thing to worry about was whether or not she would be hit with more chores and less free time. But the sick feeling in her stomach was not going away.

CHAPTER 11

Helen

Helen could barely sleep that night, and every time she drifted off, she saw the faces of Nazi soldiers looming before her, demanding her name. Maman was calling out to her, but Helen couldn't find her. And Henry was gripping her arm, his mouth open in a silent scream. What was her name? Helen couldn't remember. She was suffocating and choking. And then she would wake up, coughing and sweaty, and not wanting to close her eyes for fear that the dream would start again.

She finally gave up on sleep and sat up in bed. It didn't help that the room was stifling hot. The soft snores of the other girls filled the dark space. She pushed back the covers and got out of bed, creeping to the door and pulling it open with hardly a creak. She didn't want to wake anyone, didn't want to answer any questions about why she was up and wandering about. She didn't know if it was okay to venture from her room in the middle of the night. But she had to get some air.

The hallway felt cooler and Helen breathed in deeply, wiping the sweat from her upper lip and brushing away the curls that were stuck to her forehead. She tiptoed carefully down the staircase, holding on to the wooden railing and glancing every now and then over her shoulder. No one was about.

What now? she wondered as she reached the landing and allowed her eyes to adjust to the darkness. Perhaps a glass of water would help. Then, she might be ready to get back into bed. Dark shadows stretched across the wooden floor and up the walls as she walked toward the kitchen. It was strange to be here all alone, and to hear nothing. Normally, the halls buzzed with children running from room to room. Tonight, these dark and quiet halls reminded her of the night she and Henry had first arrived. That was just a few weeks ago, but it felt like so much longer.

Helen reached the kitchen and swung the door open. She thought for a moment about turning on a light, and then rejected the idea. She sensed she'd be in trouble if one of the nuns found her here in the middle of the night. And if that nun happened to be Sister Agnes, there was no telling what would follow. Better to make her way in the dark.

She reached the sink and turned on the water, letting the cool stream run across her hands and then bringing them up to her face. She stayed that way for a moment, pressing her hands against her cheeks and then across the back of her neck. Finally, she closed her eyes and bent forward to take a sip. Suddenly, the kitchen was flooded in light and a voice behind her asked, "What are you doing here?"

Helen whirled around, squinting in the harsh bright light. There in the doorway was a young boy.

"You scared me to death!" she cried. "I thought you were one of the nuns."

The boy had dark brown eyes and wavy brown hair that he brushed out of his eyes as he stared at Helen. There was a small smile on his lips. "Do I look like one of the nuns? Besides, only guilty people get scared when they're caught."

Now he was *sounding* like one of the nuns!

He extended his hand to her. "I'm Albert," he said. Without waiting for an invitation, he entered the kitchen, allowing the door to shut behind him, and walked up to her. His hand was still extended, waiting for Helen to grab it and return the greeting.

"Do you make a habit of sneaking up on people?" she asked, ignoring his hand. Still shaken, she brushed away the drops of water streaming down her chin and onto her nightgown.

The boy shrugged. "Sorry. I'm not used to finding anyone up in the middle of the night." He extended his hand again. "Can we start again? I'm Albert. Albert Gotlieb."

Helen had seen this boy in passing here at the convent. He was one of the older ones. She stared at his hand for a moment and then reached over to shake it. "I'm Helen."

He smiled. "Yes, Helen Rosenthal. I know your name. I'm sorry I haven't said hello to you sooner."

"Are you the welcoming committee?"

"Not exactly. But I've been here for eight months now, and I notice everything and everyone."

"Why are you up?" Helen asked.

"I'm not much of a sleeper. Never have been. The sisters know that, so they let me roam around at night. What about you?"

"I couldn't sleep either," Helen replied, feeling her heartbeat slow to normal. "I just came for some water."

Albert moved over to the icebox. He swung the door open and peered inside. "How about some milk? The sisters don't mind if I get something when I'm up. We just have to put everything away before the cook gets here in the morning." He glanced over at her. "Hide the evidence and all."

Helen hesitated. She wasn't really in the mood for company. But a glass of cool milk certainly sounded inviting. She nodded and pulled out a stool from behind the counter. By now, Albert had taken the jar of milk from the icebox, uncapped it, and poured some milk into two glasses that he had taken down from the cupboard. He slid one over to Helen and then took a seat opposite her.

She took a long sip. *Delicious!*

"I'd warm it for you, but lighting the stove in the middle of the night may bring the nuns running," Albert said.

"This is perfect." Helen allowed herself to smile for the first time. "Thank you," she added.

Albert sat back and stared at her. "So, why couldn't you sleep?"

Helen hesitated again. How much did she really want to share with this boy she had just met? Then again, why not just tell him what she was worried about? He seemed to know his way around, and perhaps he had information that might calm her fears. It was worth a try. She quickly filled him in on what had happened to her and Henry on their outing.

"Yes, I heard about what happened to you in town. Is that what's keeping you up?" he asked.

Helen nodded. "That and all this talk that the Nazis may be closer to this place than anyone had thought."

Albert shook his head. "As I said, I've been at the convent for some time now and nothing bad has happened here. I trust the nuns. They'll do whatever they need to do to keep us safe. If this place becomes dangerous, they'll move us somewhere else."

"But where?" Helen demanded. Maman had said there were no other places to go. And if they left, how would her mother ever find her? She didn't share that worry with Albert.

He shrugged his shoulders. "I've learned not to think too far into the future."

Helen sighed. "My father always said that worrying about tomorrow takes all the joy out of today. But all I ever do is worry about the future. Doesn't it scare you to think about leaving here and going somewhere else?"

Albert shrugged again. "I'm all alone, so it really doesn't matter to me where I go."

"Where are you from?"

"Vienna. When my parents were taken, I was passed around from neighbor to neighbor—the friendly ones of course, not the ones who were out to get us. I finally ended up here with a group of kids smuggled out of Austria. I have no idea what's happened to my parents. But I guess I'm luckier than many. I'm still alive."

Helen gulped. It was the kind of story she had heard from so many of the children here. "Do you have any brothers or sisters?"

Albert shook his head. "No, it's just me." He paused and then suddenly asked, "How is your brother doing? Henry, right?"

This boy knew a lot. She nodded.

Albert leaned forward and stared at her. "Seriously, though, I've noticed that he's having a hard time. I introduced myself to him a couple of days ago, but he just stared back at me. I know he's not talking."

There was nothing in Albert's eyes to suggest that he wanted to pry. His face was open and sincere. But it was unnerving to have him stare at her. She looked away, fidgeted with the sleeve of her nightgown, and scratched at a stain on the counter. Albert waited patiently without saying another word. Finally, Helen looked up at him.

"I'm worried about Henry. You're right; he doesn't talk, and after our outing to town, I'm afraid he may disappear into himself even more. I'm not sure there's anything anyone can do for him."

Albert nodded. "It took me a while before I was able to relax here—and trust anyone. I think I was a lot like your brother when I first arrived."

"But what changed for you?" Maybe Albert had some advice that would be helpful to Henry.

Albert brushed the hair from his eyes again. "I just decided that accepting my situation was better than giving up on it. And once I did that, I felt pretty strong. But Henry has to decide for himself whether he's going to fight the people who are trying to help him, or join the team."

Helen sighed; she knew that Albert was right, even though she still felt helpless about how to change Henry's mind.

"This conversation has gotten way too serious," Albert said suddenly. And then he smiled. "It's too bad the clown hasn't been here for a while. We need a show like his to lighten the mood around here."

"What clown?" Helen replied. She vaguely recalled Michelle saying something about a clown on her first day here.

"His real name is Marcel Marceau. We've just always called him the clown."

"Do you know when he's going to come back?" It would be wonderful to see a show of some kind. That could definitely help take her mind off her other worries. And she was sure that it would be good for Henry.

"Soon, I hope. Usually, he comes every week. But lately, he's been coming less often. I asked Mère Supérieure when he was coming back, but she said she didn't know." Albert suddenly smiled. "I suppose Mère Supérieure gave you a new name when you arrived," he said, switching topics. "Mine's Marc Durand. Do I look anything like a Marc to you?"

Helen laughed for the first time. "About as much as I look like Claire Rochette."

"I'll never get used to it," Albert said, shaking his head. "But I know how important it is." He gestured toward a window. "I guess you learned that firsthand."

Just then, the kitchen door swung open again and there was Sister Cecile standing in the doorway. Her mouth fell open when she saw them.

"What on earth are you doing here?" she asked, pulling a woolen shawl up to her neck. She was wearing a nightgown, and her hair, usually hidden under her wimple, lay in curls across her shoulders. It was strange to see her out of her nun's habit.

"Good morning, Sister," Albert said easily. "Or is it still the middle of the night?"

Helen stumbled to her feet. "Neither of us could sleep. And Albert said that it was okay to have some milk. It is okay, isn't it?"

Sister Cecile paused, still looking startled, and

then finally smiled. "Yes, of course, it's fine. I have trouble sleeping myself at times." She brushed her hair behind her ears.

"Would you like some milk?" Albert asked.

Sister Cecile's smile grew broader. "Perhaps another time. Thank you for the offer. Just make sure you tidy up everything before you leave. The cook might not be pleased if she comes in to a messy kitchen in the morning."

"We will, Sister," Helen replied. "And thank you."

She and Albert washed up their glasses as soon as Sister Cecile left the kitchen. Then they made their way back up the staircase. Albert hadn't answered all of her questions or lessened all her worries. But talking had definitely helped.

She paused at the top of the stairs. This time, she was the one to extend her hand. "It was good to meet you, Albert, or should I say Marc?"

He smiled and shook her hand. "You, too, Helen, aka Claire. And thanks for the company."

Helen grinned. "Thanks for the milk." And then she added, "It's a good thing it was Sister Cecile who found us."

He smiled again. "That's for sure."

Helen turned and made her way into her dorm room and into her bed. Minutes later, she was fast asleep.

CHAPTER 12

Henry

Henry didn't want to get out of bed. A week had passed since their outing to town, but he still couldn't get the sight of those Nazi soldiers out of his mind— with their shiny black boots and that ugly symbol on their arms. Everyone was so upset about the whole thing—mean Sister Agnes, Mère Supérieure with her pointy nose, even Helen. It scared him to hear them talk about soldiers getting closer. He was missing Maman and Papa more than ever now. The sadness came in waves, sometimes growing so strong that he thought his heart would explode. He didn't know missing someone could hurt like this. His mind went back and forth between missing his parents and worrying about bad things that might happen. Sad and scared; back and forth like the pendulum in the big grandfather clock that had sat in their home in Frankfurt.

So, this morning he wanted to stay put. Maybe if he pulled the covers up over his head, no one would notice him. The other boys in his room would leave and he would be all alone—maybe have a chance to do more writing in his code book. He kept the book under his bedcovers, hidden from sight, and only pulled it out when no one was around. Maybe if he wrote about that day in town and being questioned by the Nazi soldiers, he might start to feel better about it all. Writing things down helped. But he could only do that if he was left in peace and quiet. Now, the wake-up bell was ringing loudly, echoing in Henry's head. The sun was bright in his dorm room, and all around him, boys were stretching, throwing back their covers, and getting dressed. The noise level in the room was climbing. Still, Henry didn't move. He lay still, watching the action around him through narrow slits in his partly closed eyes.

The boy in the next cot—Henry knew his name was Philip—was staring at him.

"Hey, aren't you going to get up?" Philip was skinny, and taller than all the other boys in the room. His face was a bit lopsided; that was the only way to describe it. His eye and cheek on one side were higher than on the other.

Henry didn't answer.

"Are you sick or something?" Philip persisted, standing up and coming closer to Henry's bed.

Henry wanted him to go away or stop talking to him. But Philip did not leave.

"If you're not sick, then the nuns will be really mad if you don't get up."

By now, another boy had joined Philip to stand over Henry's bed. His name was Paul. He had ginger hair and the palest skin Henry had ever seen. He had a reputation for being first for everything: first to the dining hall for meals, first to classes, first to finish his chores. The two boys began to talk to one another as if Henry wasn't right there, lying in his bed beside them.

"He's only been here a few weeks," Paul said. "Maybe he doesn't know the rules yet." Paul had tried to talk to Henry a few days earlier, but Henry had walked away from him. He didn't like this boy who seemed to be in everyone's business.

"That's what I'm trying to tell him," Philip replied. "But he isn't listening to me."

"He doesn't talk much," Paul continued. "I don't think I've heard him say anything the whole time he's been here." Paul leaned down and spoke to

Henry, raising his voice. "Are you awake? Can you hear us?"

Of course he heard what they were saying. *I'm not deaf,* Henry thought. He could feel a slow burn starting in the pit of his stomach and rising to his chest. He squeezed his eyes shut and pulled the blankets up over his ears. But nothing could block out the sound of the boys talking about him.

"Do you know where he's from?" Philip asked.

"Germany, I think," Paul responded.

"How did he get here?"

"I heard one of the nuns say that his mother brought him and left him here—him and his sister."

At that, Henry began to take more notice. It was one thing for these boys to wonder why he wasn't saying anything. It was an entirely different matter when they started to talk about his family, or how he had come here. How did they know all that stuff about him when he hadn't told anyone? The slow burn of anger in his stomach was getting worse. Henry wanted the boys to stop. He felt his body coil, snakelike, ready to pounce if these boys said anything more. He tightened his grip on his blanket.

"Where's his father?" Philip asked.

Papa!

"I don't know," Paul replied. "Maybe he's dead or something."

And that was all it took. Paul may have had a reputation for being quick, but he was no match for Henry. His eyes flew open and he shot out of bed like a lightning bolt, lunging at Paul and knocking him to the ground. His arms swung in wide circles, punching Paul from all directions, and all the while he felt angry tears roll down his cheeks. This boy had said that his father might be dead. What right did he have to say that? It wasn't true. It couldn't be true. Henry wanted to scream all that and more. But instead, he continued to bash Paul with all of his might and fury. Paul raised his arms to protect himself and tried desperately to push Henry off him. But there was nothing he could do.

In the background, Henry could hear other boys gathering around, some shouting at him to stop, others yelling for help, a few encouraging Paul to fight back. And then suddenly, strong arms appeared out of nowhere and wrapped themselves around Henry's body, pulling him away from Paul.

"Hey, stop it," a male voice commanded. "It's enough!"

Henry looked over his shoulder, recognizing the boy holding him back. His name was Albert, and he had tried to talk to him a couple of times. Albert was one of the older ones, and the other boys looked up to him.

Henry struggled in Albert's arms for a few more seconds, but Albert was much stronger. Finally, Henry let his arms fall to his sides, though his fists remained firmly clenched. He breathed heavily and swallowed hard, staring at Paul, who slowly raised himself from the ground.

"Somebody needs to tell me what's going on," Albert demanded. "You boys know there's no fighting here."

Albert questioned Paul and Philip and the other boys, piecing together what had happened and how things had gotten out of control. The boys answered his questions like he was one of the nuns. Henry stood listening to the interrogation. He didn't care that everyone was talking except him. He didn't care that the facts were unfolding without him. By now, his tears had dried up. The fury he had been feeling was gone, released like smoke through a chimney. Instead, he was feeling just as sad and just as scared as he had felt when he opened his eyes that morning.

When Albert finished with the boys, he sent them downstairs to breakfast. Paul walked past Henry, glaring at him and rubbing his cheek, where a red welt had appeared. The skin around his left eye was already starting to change color, going from pale pink to a deep, dark purple. When all the boys were gone, Albert turned to face Henry.

"Okay, Henry, it's just you and me now," Albert began. "Do you think you're ready to say something?"

Henry hung his head.

"I get it. You don't want to talk." Albert leaned forward. "I know it's hard for you to be here."

Henry still couldn't look at Albert.

"Do you think your parents would want you to go around punching other boys?"

Henry squeezed his eyes shut. His parents would never have liked that he was fighting.

"Listen, it was hard for me when I came here, too. I was really scared, and mad at everyone. But you need to realize that it's also hard for all the boys in here. They also miss their parents."

Henry looked up at Albert, unblinking. He just couldn't bring himself to feel bad for the other boys. No one understood just how much he needed Maman and Papa.

"My parents are both gone," Albert continued. "I have no idea where they are. At least you know where your mother is. And your sister is here with you. That makes you so much luckier than most of the rest of us."

Henry frowned. He hadn't thought of himself as lucky at all.

"We're all just trying to help one another," Albert continued. "Can't you see that?"

There was something in what Albert was saying that made Henry think. Maybe he really was better off than most of the other children here.

"It would be so much easier for you if you leaned on us a bit," Albert added.

Henry lowered his eyes and looked away. He thought that no one understood him. But maybe Albert was someone who could. And maybe Henry *could* talk to Albert about all the sad and angry thoughts in his head.

Suddenly Sister Cecile rushed into the dorm room. Henry had never seen her look so upset.

"The boys told me there was a fight of some kind," she cried.

Albert smiled easily at the nun. "Everything's under control, Sister. Our friend here was just having a hard morning."

Sister Cecile stared at Henry and then over at Albert. "How hard?"

"Let's just say that Paul might end up with quite a shiner."

Sister Cecile sighed deeply. "Thank you, Albert," she said. "I'll take over from here."

Albert nodded, but before leaving the room, he placed a hand on Henry's shoulder. "Remember what I said, Henry. You don't have any enemies here at the convent." With that, he walked out of the dorm.

Sister Cecile stood looking at Henry for a long time before she finally began to talk. "We are all trying very hard to understand how you are feeling. But you can't go around attacking people, no matter how frustrated you are."

Henry lowered his head again. He knew Sister Cecile was just trying to help. Albert was trying to help. Even Helen was trying to help. He still felt completely miserable.

"You were lucky it was Albert walking by your dorm room this morning, and not one of the other nuns," she said.

Henry nodded.

"I have to punish you for this outburst. I have no choice." Sister Cecile pulled her shoulders back and inhaled deeply. "You will stay after class today and you will write 'I will not hit anyone' on the blackboard one hundred times. Do you understand me?"

When he looked up at Sister Cecile, he almost thought she was smiling.

"Now get dressed and go downstairs for breakfast before someone realizes you're not there." She turned and walked out of the room.

Now that he was alone, part of him *was* grateful that Albert was the one who had come across the fight, and not someone like Sister Agnes. She would have made him mop the floors or clean the windows for a week. Writing lines was easy. He could write a million lines. It still wouldn't change the way he was feeling.

He dressed slowly. But before leaving his dorm room, he searched under his blanket and brought out his code book. Then he sat down on his bed, reached for a pencil, and began to write.

CHAPTER 13

Helen

A couple of mornings later, Mère Supérieure announced at breakfast that all future outings to town had been canceled. It came as no surprise to Helen. She had been aware of the many discussions that were taking place between the nuns as they scurried off after every meal to meet behind closed doors. At least there had been no talk of her and Henry being sent away from the convent.

She caught up with Albert after breakfast as they were leaving the dining hall. They hung back from the other children so that they could have a conversation.

"I heard you broke up a fight that Henry started," Helen began.

"Standing up for himself is a good thing. It means Henry hasn't given up. He just needs to learn to channel some of that in a better way. Fistfighting is going to get him in more trouble."

"I know. I'm still so worried about him." Helen couldn't remember when he had gone this long without talking.

"After the fight, I thought Henry was going to talk to me," Albert said. "But then Sister Cecile showed up."

"I had hoped the outing to town might open him up—let him see that things were okay here." But of course, the outing had been disastrous, and instead of making Henry feel more secure, it had closed him down even more. It scared everyone. "I don't really care about outings anymore," Helen added. "I can't believe I'm saying this, but I just don't want to leave this place right now."

"I know what you mean," Albert replied. "But it's not just this town that's been invaded by Nazis. A few weeks ago, Adolf Hitler's troops marched into Paris. They practically wiped out the entire French army. And they killed almost a hundred thousand French soldiers." Albert went on to explain that since then,

France and Germany had signed an agreement to stop fighting, but it meant that Nazi Germany would occupy nearly all of France.

Helen sucked in her breath. "How do you know all of that?"

Albert shrugged. "I overheard the nuns talking."

Albert seemed to hear things that no one else was aware of; Helen didn't know how. But she was grateful for the information.

"We're in the southern part of France," Albert continued. "This area is called the free zone. It's still a safe place."

Helen wasn't convinced. "How safe can it be when Hitler controls the rest of the country?" She was suddenly overcome with a deep longing for her parents. There was still no word from Maman, and it had been so many weeks. When some of the other children received letters from their loved ones, Helen would retreat to her dorm room. At those times, it was easier to be alone than to watch the joy on the faces of the others who squealed with delight as they tore open letters and devoured the news from home.

Mère Supérieure continued to insist that it was not unusual for long periods of time to go by before parents would be able to contact their children. The letters that did arrive were somehow smuggled into the convent through some mysterious network of friends. Helen knew nothing more than that. But perhaps that was why Maman hadn't sent something yet, she thought. Maybe Maman hadn't found a sympathetic contact to bring a letter for her and Henry. "Look around you," the head had nun said. "Some of the children here have not heard from their parents in close to a year."

A year! In a year, Helen was afraid that she would begin to forget what her mother even looked like. Already, her mental image of her father was fading. How bushy was his mustache? How big were the muscles in his arms? Had the frames of his glasses been round or square? She closed her eyes and conjured up the mental photograph of Maman—the lifted eyebrow, the freckle by the side of her mouth, her full, red lips. *She's still there. I can still see her,* Helen thought. Seeing Maman in her mind helped. But it wasn't enough.

Helen didn't say any of this to Albert. It would be insensitive of her to moan about letters from home when she knew that Albert didn't know anything about where his parents were. Instead, she said, "I'm going up to Henry's room. I'm hoping I can get him to eat something." She pointed down to the napkin she was holding. She had wrapped up some fresh bread slathered with raspberry jam, the kind that he had always loved. Not only was Henry still not talking, he also seemed to be growing thinner by the day. It was as if he was completely disappearing.

"Just don't let Sister Agnes catch you taking food out of the dining hall," Albert replied.

At the thought of Sister Agnes, Helen groaned. For a while after their disastrous outing, she had managed to escape the mean nun's notice. But just the other day, when she thought she was in the clear, Sister Agnes had stopped her on the staircase.

"You were late for class yesterday," Sister Agnes had said, her face puckered as if she had swallowed vinegar.

"I can explain, Sister," Helen stammered, her heart sinking. "I wasn't feeling well yesterday—the beginning of a cold, I think. I went back to my room to get some tissues and—"

"And then you were late," Sister Agnes interrupted.

"Yes, but I didn't mean to be. I just wasn't feeling well …" Her voice trailed off as she braced herself for what was to follow.

Sister Agnes folded her arms and inhaled sharply. "One who is good at excuses is rarely good at anything else."

"But Sister, if you'd just let me—"

"Enough!" Sister Agnes cut her off. Helen had to spend the afternoon pulling weeds in the garden.

She showed her cut and swollen fingers to Albert,

comforted by his sympathetic nod. "Michelle said that the extra chores would stop after a while. But I still feel as if I'm the only one that Sister Agnes goes after. Maybe working in the garden was really a punishment for talking to the Nazi soldiers."

"Maybe," Albert agreed. "Just try to stay out of her way."

"Easier said than done!"

Helen said good-bye to Albert and was heading for Henry's room when she passed Sister Cecile. She tried to hide the bread she was taking to Henry behind her back. But the nun stopped her.

"Is there something there that I should see?" Sister Cecile asked.

Reluctantly, Helen pulled the napkin out to show the nun. "It's for Henry," she explained. "I'm trying to get him to eat something."

Sister Cecile paused, looked around and over her shoulder, and then nodded. "I think that's a very good idea. But go quickly, before anyone else catches you."

"Thank you, Sister." Helen beamed. She was about to continue walking when she paused again. "Sister Cecile, can I ask you something?"

"Of course," the nun replied.

Helen took a deep breath. "It's about Sister Agnes."

Sister Cecile hesitated, and her eyes clouded over with something that Helen didn't quite understand.

Was it fear? Helen ignored the look, took another breath, and plowed on. "I feel like Sister Agnes is punishing me all the time."

Sister Cecile nodded cautiously. "Sister Agnes is focused on building character and making you strong. I know she has a particular … um … style, but she wouldn't ask you to do anything she didn't think you could handle."

"It's not that I can't do the things she tells me to do, it's just that I think she hates me. And I don't know why."

"Oh, that's not true! Sister Agnes worries about you and everyone here."

That's just what Mère Supérieure had said. But Sister Agnes sure had a strange way of showing her concern, Helen thought. "I was wondering, do you think you could talk to Sister Agnes? Maybe ask her to be a little easier on me?" Sister Cecile had said that she was here for Helen if she needed anything. Now was the time to ask for help.

But instead of responding with a decisive "of course!" Sister Cecile hesitated again, shifting from one foot to the other. She looked down and then away, avoiding eye contact with Helen.

"I don't think I'm the one who can do that," she finally stuttered.

Why not? Helen wondered. Wasn't she a nun, like

all the others? Why couldn't she ask one of her sister nuns to be kinder?

"I understand how you're feeling. And I truly want to help," Sister Cecile continued, finally looking up at Helen's face. "But I can't."

Helen's heart sank. Sister Cecile was the only person who had offered her help. *I'm here for you if you need me*, she had said. But the one time Helen had asked for something, Sister Cecile had turned her down. Helen's shoulders sagged and she turned away from the nun.

"I-I'm sorry," Sister Cecil stammered. "You must try to be grateful just to be here."

"I *am* grateful," Helen interrupted. "But it's not about—"

"Just try and stay out of Sister Agnes's way. That's really all I can offer."

And with that, Sister Cecile turned and walked away. It wasn't at all what Helen had hoped for, especially from this nun who seemed so concerned. Helen sighed and continued up the stairs, wondering for the hundredth or possibly the millionth time when Sister Agnes would finally leave her alone.

CHAPTER 14

Henry

He was making a list in his code book. The list was called "Things I would do if I was home right now." Each item was numbered carefully.

1. Go to the park with Papa and kick a soccer ball.

Henry paused. He usually scored all the goals when they played together, even though he knew that Papa just let him win. They would come home sweaty and tired, and Maman would make him take a bath before he was allowed to do anything else. She said he looked as if he had been rolling in mud, which was probably true. You couldn't score goals if you weren't ready to slide in the dirt. The trips to the park had ended when the law that said Jewish people couldn't go to public parks anymore was passed.

2. Build a fort with Ernest.

That made Henry pause again. His friend Ernest had stopped playing with him weeks before they had left their home to go to Kronberg. Henry still had a hard time understanding this. They had known each other since before they could even walk or talk. Maman and Ernest's mother had become friends before the two boys were even born. When Maman had found out that Ernest wasn't allowed to play with Henry, she had been furious, angrier than when Henry had broken her favorite china tea pot. She had marched over to Ernest's house to have a word with his mother. Henry had watched eagerly for her return by the front window, ready to go out and start building a fort with Ernest as soon as Maman had fixed things. Maybe he and Ernest would add their small wooden soldiers to the fort, pretending that they were defending it from enemies. But his mother had returned home looking white and shaken. She wouldn't say a word about what had happened at

Ernest's house, not even when Henry had begged her to tell him. Finally, she had just looked at him and said, "You'll find another friend, Henry, my love."

But there had been no other friends, and Henry had stopped playing with his wooden soldiers. And soon after that, Papa had been taken, and then they had run from their home. And now he was here in this awful place, feeling completely lost.

A couple of boys suddenly entered the dorm room. They were laughing and shoving one another, but stopped short when they saw Henry. He shut his code book and quickly shoved it under his blanket just as the boys approached his cot.

"Hey, you're Henry, right?" one boy said. He was about Henry's age, with short-cropped dark hair and glasses that had slipped down to the end of his nose. He and the boy with him came from one of the other dorms. What were they doing in his room?

"He doesn't talk," the other boy said. When this boy spoke, Henry could see that his front two teeth were missing. He spoke with a soft lisp. "Remember, the other guys told us about that."

The boys in his dorm room had been talking about him—probably talking about the fight he'd been in. That didn't surprise Henry. But he wondered what else they had said.

"Are you sick? Is that why you're not talking?" the first boy asked as he pushed his glasses back up on his nose.

Henry stared evenly at him, wishing that he and his friend would leave so that he could go back to his code book. The last time someone refused to leave him alone, there had been trouble. Henry did not want to start a fight again. But it seemed that these two were not yet ready to go.

"He's just like the clown," the first boy said, turning to his friend. "He doesn't talk either. But at least his shows are funny."

"Yeah," the boy with missing teeth replied, nodding at Henry. "You'll probably like the clown."

A clown that doesn't talk? That sounded interesting. Henry had only seen a clown once in his life, when Papa had taken the family to the Circus Sarrasani in Dresden. The show had been held under a gigantic white tent, and there had been tumblers and acrobats and horses, and elephants, too, more than twenty of them! And, of course, there had been a troupe of clowns. Some of them had painted their faces white and wore pointy hats and big, colorful costumes. They had ran through the aisles doing silly things to make the audience laugh, like tripping over their big shoes or squirting water in each other's faces.

Henry wondered if this clown would be anything like that.

The two boys stood for another moment looking at Henry, until the one with glasses grabbed the other by the arm. "Let's get out of here." He looked back at Henry. "Maybe you'll say something next time we see you," he said as he and his friend ran from the room.

Henry exhaled. *Finally*, he thought as he retrieved his code book from under his blanket. He grabbed his pencil and was about to continue his list when there was a soft knock on the dorm room door. *What now?* He looked up to see Helen standing in the doorway. He quickly shut his code book and once again shoved it under his blanket.

Helen walked toward his bed, glancing at the blanket as if she knew something was under there. She didn't say a word, just held something out to him.

"Here," she said. "I brought you something to eat."

Henry stared at the napkin she held in her hand, but made no move to take it. He frowned at her, annoyed. Writing the list had made him feel better— even when he thought about Ernest. His important writing had already been interrupted once today. And now, his sister had interrupted him again. In that moment, he just wanted her to leave.

But Helen wasn't going anywhere. She stood in

front of him, her hand extended. And when Henry did not reach out to take the napkin, she unfolded it, revealing a big piece of crusty white bread, slathered in jam. Some of the jam had seeped out and into the napkin, which was now bright red.

"You need to eat something, Henry," Helen said, still holding the food out to him. She had that worried look on her face. "Are you still not going to say anything to me?"

He looked away. He hated it when his sister looked so upset. But there was nothing he was willing to do about that. Staying quiet was still better than talking, at least for now.

Finally, Helen sighed. "Okay, I'll just leave this here. Maybe you'll eat it later." She folded the bread back into the napkin and put it down on his cot.

Once she'd left the room, closing the door softly behind her, Henry looked down at the napkin, oozing with red jam. It was the kind he liked. He reached over, opened it slowly, broke off a piece of bread, and placed it in his mouth, chewing carefully. It was sweet and delicious. It reminded him of the time he and Helen had gone to their backyard to pick raspberries from the bush that Maman had planted. He and Helen had eaten so many, there were hardly any left to bring indoors. He couldn't remember a time when he had laughed so much with his sister. Finally, Henry reached under his blanket for his code book and pulled it out, staring at the list of things he would do if he were at home. He picked up his pencil and held it above the page, pausing for a moment longer. And then finally he wrote,

3. Do something special with Helen.

CHAPTER 15

Helen

The clown was finally coming to the convent! The air was practically vibrating with energy. Maybe it was because everyone had been cooped up inside the convent for weeks now, but the idea of someone coming in—someone Michelle said was a performer and a friend—just perked everyone up. Even Sister Agnes looked happy! She was bouncing from table to table in the dining hall, urging everyone to hurry up and finish their lunch as quickly as possible and then clear the tables and chairs. There was a grin plastered across her face that, at first, took Helen aback. A sneering Sister Agnes was what she was accustomed to. This beaming Sister Agnes was almost alarming.

"Tell me again who he is?" Helen asked Michelle as they began to push tables to the side of the great hall and line up the chairs in rows.

"His name is Marcel. That's what the sisters call him. But we call him the clown."

A clown! It had been so long since Helen had seen a clown—or a show of any kind.

"And you said he's been here before." Helen wasn't sure how a clown, who she'd only seen in circuses, could perform in the convent.

Michelle nodded. "He doesn't wear makeup or a costume, or anything like that."

Helen frowned. "That doesn't sound like a clown at all."

Michelle sighed. "His shows are great. But it's better if you just wait and see for yourself."

Now Helen was really curious. She felt herself caught up in the excitement along with everyone else. Besides, any change from the usual routine was worth getting excited about. She and the other children finished setting up the great hall and took their seats. The chatter in the room was beginning to reach a fever pitch when Mère Supérieure led the other nuns into the hall and walked to the front. She raised her hand to signal silence and waited for the children to settle and turn their attention to her.

"Children, I know it's been hard for you not to be able to leave the convent these last few weeks. And I know most of you are worried about events that have happened outside these walls.

"The sisters and I will continue to do our best to keep you safe. But we also want you to try and enjoy yourselves here as well. We know that's also important. So you are all in for a great treat," she said. "Some of you have already had the pleasure of watching this young man perform for us. For others, this will be a new experience. But I can assure you that it will be a wonderful experience for all. It gives me great pleasure to introduce our special guest, Monsieur Marcel Marceau."

A back door opened and Helen twisted in her seat, craning her neck to catch a glimpse of the visitor. He strode in, making his way to the front of the room as the children clapped, cheered, and stomped their feet. Once at the front, he waved his arm above his head and then swept it down and across his chest, leaning forward in a deep, long bow. As he stood back up, Helen could see that he was young, seventeen, maybe eighteen at the most, with a full head of wiry, dark hair, a long nose, and intense eyes. He wore a tight, striped T-shirt and oversized overalls held up with suspenders. Finally, he raised his hand and the room grew quiet.

Without saying a word, the clown struck a pose. And then, one hand began to snap back and forth in the air, as if he were cracking a whip. The other hand was held straight out in front of him, as if he were clutching something. *What is it that's he's pretending to hold?* Helen wondered. And then she got it. It was an imaginary small chair that he thrust forward and then pulled back.

"I've seen him do this before," Michelle whispered, leaning over to Helen. "He's pretending to be a lion tamer."

Of course! Now it all made sense. The clown strutted around a make-believe ring, snapping his imaginary whip and thrusting his invisible chair. Then suddenly, he froze, and his eyes grew round with fear. It was as if the lion had suddenly entered the ring. The children screamed as the clown first confronted the lion, shaking his head, jutting his chin out in front of him, and pretending to force the lion to sit on its haunches and then stand up. It was as if he had figured out a way to tame the lion, confront the wild beast, and take charge. After each trick he made the lion do, he bowed deeply to the audience, who showed their appreciation with more applause and more cheers. Next, the clown appeared to force the lion to stand still. He laid his pretend whip and chair on the ground, turned his back on the lion, and began to walk away, parading proudly. Once again, the children screamed and pointed to the empty air behind the clown, as if the lion were really there and about to pounce.

Helen was mesmerized. The clown was so convincing and his performance so lifelike that she could have sworn there actually was a lion in the room! And he did all of this without making a sound—not one word. She screamed and roared with laughter along with everyone else as the clown looked over his shoulder, saw that the lion was coming after him, and began to run in circles around the room as if he were just steps ahead of the lion's jaws.

On and on the performance went. At one point, the clown began to pry the jaws of the make-believe lion open, and then he stuck his head inside the animal's mouth, showing once more that he was in charge. That was perhaps the best moment of the entire show, and the clown was rewarded with more cheers and applause.

And then, all too soon as far as Helen was concerned, it was over. The clown swept his arm across his chest and bowed deeply once more while the children jumped to their feet to show their appreciation. Even the nuns were beaming and applauding.

Helen glanced around for Henry and spotted him sitting by himself on the other side of the room. She wasn't surprised to see him all alone. Henry had no friends at the convent. What shocked her was the look on his face. His eyes were as round as two coins and he was beaming. Helen hadn't seen such absolute and total joy on his face since they had been together in Frankfurt as one complete family.

Helen watched as the children surrounded the clown, chattering in delight. As she stood to leave, she saw that Henry remained in his seat, still beaming, his feet swinging back and forth with a nervous kind of energy. Helen wanted to go over and talk to him, but she was afraid she might spoil the moment—burst this bubble of delight that seemed to have possessed him. She gazed at her brother for another moment. Then, with a sigh, she began to walk out of the room. At the door, she paused, looking back over her shoulder to see Henry staring at the clown. The clown was staring back at Henry.

CHAPTER 16

Henry

Without saying one word, this clown had grabbed Henry's attention and wrapped him up in a complete story. He had never seen anything like this in his life, and it lit him up. It was as if an electrical surge had just passed through his body, jump-starting something that had felt dead for so long.

When the show was over, Henry stayed in his seat, watching the clown greet the children who had rushed over to *ooh* and *ahh* and gush over him. Everyone was asking questions: "How did you do that part with the lion's jaws?" "Where do you get your ideas?" "When did you learn how to do this?" The clown was patient, listening to every question and taking the time to answer. Henry also wanted to walk up to him and ask how he could do those things with his body—how he could entertain everyone, how he could say so much without saying a word.

One by one, the other children left the room. Helen, who had waited behind for a few minutes, also walked out. Finally, it was just Henry and the clown. And that's when all of his excitement and eagerness drained out of his body. How could he ever talk to this person? How was he going to be able to tell him how much he had enjoyed—no, how much he had *loved*—the show? He was still not sure how to begin to open up. He didn't even know why he hadn't left the hall. All he knew was that he wanted to be close to this young man, maybe figure out how the clown could "talk" to people in silence? That was something Henry could definitely use.

Another long minute passed while Henry sat staring at the clown, and the clown gazed back at him. Then suddenly, the clown began to walk toward him. Henry sat higher in his chair. His legs, which had been swinging back and forth, went still. His body stiffened.

Closer and closer the clown came until he stood directly in front of Henry, peering down at him, not making a sound. Henry leaned his head back in his chair and looked up at the clown. And then, something came over him. Without saying a word, Henry rose from his chair and swept his right arm high into the air and then across his body as he bowed deeply and dramatically, just as the clown had done. He stayed like that, bent over, arm across his chest, and then rose and once again stared at the clown.

A smile began to tug at the corners of the clown's mouth. He nodded his approval and bowed as well with a dramatic sweep of his arm and a deep, forward plunge of his body. When he stood up, he was smiling broadly. Henry beamed back.

Next, the clown placed his hands in front of his face. When he moved his hands up, his face had a big grin plastered across it. When he moved his hands down, the smile turned into a giant frown. Up and down his hands moved, while his face went from grinning to scowling. Then he lowered his hands and stared once more at Henry, inviting him to give it a try.

Hesitantly at first, Henry brought his hands up to cover his face and then began to move them up and down, smiling and frowning behind his hands just as the clown had done. The clown applauded softly.

What next? Henry wondered. He didn't want this time to end. He felt as if the clown understood him, and Henry wanted to continue their quiet conversation.

And that's when the clown held his arms out in front of him and placed one hand on top of the other. He spread his fingers wide and began to roll his hands up and down like waves on the sea. At first, Henry was puzzled. What was the clown trying to do? Was he swimming? Was he pushing something away with his hands? And then a moment later, he got it. It was a bird! The clown had created an imaginary bird with his hands, one that was about to take flight. Henry watched as the clown continued to roll his hands up and down, spreading his fingers as wide as he could to create wings. And then, the bird took off. It flew high above the clown's head and swooped in big circles around his body. It even landed for a moment on Henry's shoulder, fluttering its wings before settling there lightly. Then it soared again, sweeping across the air, back and forth, up and down, until the clown released the bird, watching it continue to fly. Finally, the clown's hands came to rest at his sides.

Henry looked down at his own hands and then slowly and tentatively brought them together, spreading his fingers as the clown had done and letting his hands rise and fall. At first, his motions were clumsy. *This doesn't look like a bird at all*, he thought. It looked more like a machine, stiff and awkward. The clown reached out, helping to guide Henry's hands forward and back. And slowly but surely, Henry's hands became more fluid, rippling up and down as if the bones in his fingers had dissolved. He had created a bird and he could make it fly and swoop just as the clown had done.

Finally, he, too, brought his hands to rest at his sides. The clown nodded once more, then bowed deeply, turned, and left the room.

CHAPTER 17

Helen

The clown returned to the convent two more times in the following weeks. And at the end of each performance, Helen noticed that Henry stayed behind. Clearly, the clown had sparked something in her brother that livened him up. Wandering by his dorm room on the way to class one morning, she caught him practicing some movements that the clown must have taught him. She had hidden behind the door to his room and watched him fluttering his fingers as if there were a flock of butterflies all around his head. Another time, she caught him pretending to be a high-wire acrobat, balancing along an imaginary tightrope and holding a make-believe umbrella to keep his balance. Henry was good! She marveled at him.

She never said a word to him about watching him practice; she was afraid if she told him how good he was, she would break this magical spell that seemed to have finally captured her brother. But she did mention all of this to Albert one afternoon after the clown had finished performing and the children were filing from the room. Her brother had remained in the great hall to help put the tables and chairs back in place. Helen figured that was when the clown worked with him.

"Have you noticed anything different about Henry?" she asked.

Albert nodded. "Definitely! He's smiling. I guess he's finally accepted the fact that he needs to be here."

"But it's also the clown," Helen said. "I think he's teaching Henry how to do his tricks and skits. He still isn't talking, but between that and the writing he's doing ..."

"Writing?"

Helen hesitated before replying. While she was pretty sure that Henry wouldn't like it if he knew she watched him practicing his movements, she was absolutely certain he wouldn't want anyone to know about his writing. But Albert was her friend and someone to confide it. "He hasn't shown me any of it. But I think he writes in this notebook that he keeps under his blankets. He hides it from me whenever I walk into his dorm room. You won't say anything, will you?"

Albert smiled. "My lips are sealed. I'm just glad your brother is doing better."

"I figure it helps him to write things down." If writing and acting were the key to helping Henry, that was good enough for now.

The next time the clown returned to perform at the convent, Helen took the chance to thank him for what he was doing for her brother. Henry hadn't been able to stay behind that day. He had chores that pulled him away from the hall.

"Excuse me, Monsieur," she said, after the other children had finished asking their questions and she could finally have a moment to talk to him alone.

"Please call me Marcel," he replied.

Helen nodded shyly. "Marcel." She figured they were only a few years apart in age, but he had a way of speaking that made him seem so much older and wiser than his years. "I think you're brilliant," Helen gushed.

Marcel laughed. "Well, that may be an exaggeration. But thank you for the compliment."

Helen felt her cheeks grow warm. "And thank you

for helping my brother," she said. "I believe you've been teaching him. He seems ... happier these days."

Marcel looked puzzled.

"My brother. Henry."

Marcel's eyes lit up. "Ah yes, your brother is the quiet one. I'm glad I've helped. He has quite a flair for these movements."

"I had hoped somebody might get him to talk, but this is pretty good for now." Helen wanted to know more. "Could you tell me how you learned to do all those things?"

"It's called mime," the clown interjected.

"Yes, can you tell me how you learned to mime?"

"Have you ever heard of the American actor Charlie Chaplin?" he asked.

"Of course!" Charlie Chaplin was a world-famous silent film star. Helen's parents had once taken her to see a Charlie Chaplin silent film called *City Lights*. In it, he played a shabbily dressed little beggar who wandered the streets of a big city and found a young blind girl, with whom he fell in love. But the girl mistook him for a wealthy man and he went along with that deception, even though he worried that if she ever found out he was poor, she would leave him. The movie had a happy ending, of course, when the girl's sight was restored and she realized that even though he was poor, she had fallen in love with him.

"I was inspired by watching Chaplin and how he could create stories without words," Marcel said. "I realized that I was born to be a mime, just like a fish is born to be in the water and a bird is born to fly. Would you like me to teach you something as well?" he asked. "*Le muet* has become quite accomplished."

Le muet? Who is that? Helen wondered.

Marcel caught her puzzled stare. "Your brother— the quiet one. I've named him *le muet*, the one who doesn't talk—the mute."

Helen laughed softly. "It's a perfect name," she said.

"I mean it with the greatest respect," Marcel continued. "You may want him to talk, but I understand that you don't always need words to communicate." He paused. "So how about it? Are you ready to let me teach you something as well?"

Helen squirmed and looked away. Acting had never been her strong suit. She didn't even like to sing in public. "I don't think I'd be very good at it," she said.

Marcel persisted. "Just give it a try." And then he began to act out a scene in front of her in which he pretended to be walking a dog on a leash. The imaginary dog was not very cooperative. It yanked him first in one direction and then the other, throwing him completely off-balance and sending Helen into a fit of laughter. She could almost see the dog at the end of the make-believe leash. Marcel invited her to stand next to him as he demonstrated how to act as though you are being tugged around the room and how to make the audience believe something was actually pulling you. But try as she might, Helen could not get the actions. She was stiff and awkward. There was nothing fluid about her movements and nothing convincing about her acting, no matter how much guidance Marcel gave her.

"Never mind," he finally said. "You keep practicing, and before long, you'll be able to do this as well as your brother."

CHAPTER 18

Helen

A few days later, Helen was sitting in the dining hall with Michelle when Sister Cecile approached. "I need you and your brother to come with me," she said. "Mère Supérieure would like to meet with you both."

Helen's mouth went dry. Why did the head nun want to see her?

Helen glanced at Michelle, who gave her an anxious nod. Then she rose from the table. She looked across the room at Henry, caught his eye, and motioned for him to meet her in the hallway. Henry continued to look so much brighter than he had in the preceding weeks, especially right after the performances from the clown. But when he joined Helen outside the dining hall and she told him they were to meet with Mère Supérieure, Henry's face fell instantly.

Together, they walked the long hallway toward the head nun's office. The door was closed, and Helen took a deep breath and knocked. A moment later, she and Henry were seated in front of Mère Supérieure, staring apprehensively at the head nun.

"It's been some time since our last ... meeting," Mère Supérieure began. "I wanted to know how you have been."

Helen looked up at the painting of Jesus behind the sister's head. Weeks earlier, when they had first arrived, this painting had seemed so foreign to her. Now, it was strangely calming.

"Well?" Mère Supérieure asked again.

Helen clenched her fists into a ball. There were still nights when she couldn't sleep, when she dreamed about Nazi soldiers or Papa being arrested, or when she worried about Henry and what was going to happen to them. Should she say something about all of that to Mère Supérieure? In the end, she chose to say nothing.

"We're very grateful to be here, Mère Supérieure. Aren't we, Henry?" She looked at her brother, whose face was once again so low on his chest that she couldn't see his eyes.

"Andre," Mère Supérieure said.

"Pardon me?" Helen asked.

"Andre," the head nun repeated. "It would be better if you became accustomed to using your brother's new name, as well as your own. By now, you should understand the importance of remembering that."

Helen gulped. She opened her mouth to say something, but the head nun raised her hand to stop her.

"That's not the reason I've brought you in here," Mère Supérieure said.

The pounding began in Helen's chest. *What now?* She held her breath as Mère Supérieure reached into a desk drawer.

"I have these for you." The head nun pulled out two letters and extended them to Helen and to Henry, who raised his head for the first time since they had entered the office. "They are from your mother."

Helen started to reach her hands out to the nun, but then they froze in midair.

Maman!

Mère Supérieure placed an envelope in Helen's extended hand. For a moment, she began to shake so uncontrollably, she thought she might drop it. But then, she grabbed it and held it up to her face to see if she could smell something of her mother—a hint of the perfume that she used to wear or a whiff of the soap that she bathed with. There was nothing.

"You're free to take the letters with you and read them privately," Mère Supérieure was saying. "Naturally, you'll have to return them to me as soon as you can. It would be too dangerous for all of us if anyone were to come into the convent and find them. Sadly, I must destroy all the letters that arrive here."

Henry sat holding his letter unopened in his hands. Mère Supérieure had returned to some work on her desk. But Helen could not stop herself. She tore open the envelope and pulled the letter from inside. Everything around her—Mère Supérieure, Henry, the painting of Jesus—all disappeared as Helen unfolded the letter and began to read.

My darling child,
Oh, how I have missed you! Your face is in my mind and my heart every minute of every day that passes by—from the moment I rise until the moment I fall asleep. I am still here in Kronberg, and I am doing well, thanks to the generosity of this family. So far, there has been no news from your Papa. I pray that he is safe and that he will return soon. There are such terrible things happening in our country and in countries all around us. But we can't give up hope.

I am also praying that you are well, my darling girl.
I hope you are making friends at the convent. And
I hope you are taking care of your brother. He needs
you now more than ever.

I know you have had to grow up so fast—too fast!
But you are smart and you are strong. And I pray
for the day that we will be reunited.

With all my love,
Maman

Helen sat holding the letter up close to her face, still oblivious to everything around her. For a moment, it felt as if Maman were right there, standing in front of her, talking to her, reassuring her. And then, slowly, the room began to come into focus and Helen lowered the letter.

Henry still sat next to her, unmoving. His letter lay in his hands. He was just staring at it. When he turned to look up at Helen, his eyes were impossibly sad. Helen looked away.

That was when Mère Supérieure cleared her throat and said, "That's all. You may go now."

CHAPTER 19

Henry

Henry sat on his bed in his dorm room, turning the letter over and over in his hands. He couldn't believe his ears when Mère Supérieure had said that the letters were from Maman. But instead of feeling happy that his mother had written, Henry felt himself pulled down into that deep black hole where his mind had been living for such a long time, ever since his mother had left him here with Helen.

He had to admit that in the last few weeks, he had actually begun to feel better. He no longer woke up in the morning with his head so thick and heavy, he wanted to bury it underneath the blankets and never get up. He walked with his head a little higher and his eyes more open. It was Marcel who had helped him climb out of that dark place. Henry thought of him only as the clown.

At each performance, Henry was the first one in his seat and the last one to rise at the end of the show. After everyone else had left, the two of them would put the chairs back in place. Then the clown would say, "Come, *mon petit muet*. It's time to get to work." That was the name that the clown had given him, a name he didn't mind at all. And that's when the clown would begin to teach Henry all of his special movements.

Henry's favorite was pretending to be stuck in a cage with no way out. He would reach his hands up to a make-believe ceiling and then move them against sides that didn't exist. Then he would pretend that the walls of the cage were closing in on him and he would have to squeeze through an imaginary opening so that he could get free.

"Keep your hands very flat," the clown instructed, extending his arms and bending his wrists so that his hands pointed straight up, as stiff as two wooden boards. "And keep your fingers wide open, like this." The clown spread his fingers apart to demonstrate. "Now, hold your breath, squeeze your eyes shut, and lean forward. That way, your audience will think you are using all your energy to push against a real wall."

Henry nodded and repeated the movement until the clown finally said, "Well done, *petit muet*. You're becoming a real mime artist."

That was the best moment of all! And when each session was over, Henry would run to his dorm room, pull out his code book, and draw pictures of the birds and butterflies and tightrope walkers he had just created. And then, at the bottom of the page, he wrote, *I am a mime artist.*

In between visits, Henry practiced the movements over and over, smoothing out any awkward or stiff actions and trying to make each scene as perfect as the clown's. Even the way he moved his face was important—a look of surprise or fear to go along with whatever action he was performing. He knew that sometimes Helen watched him while he worked on his skits. He could sense she was nearby, hiding in the shadows of a dark hallway or peeking out from behind a door. He didn't really mind that she spied on him, as long as she didn't say anything about it to him. It would have been unbearable if she'd spoken to him or asked him what he was doing, or even complimented him. But watching from a distance was okay.

Maybe she could even see how happy he was these days. He didn't mind so much that he had not made friends with any of the other children at the convent. He didn't care if others looked at him strangely or stayed away from him completely because he didn't speak. Who needed to speak when you could act out such wonderful scenes and everyone would know exactly what you were doing and what you were saying? Between his code book and these movements, maybe he'd never have to speak again.

But the arrival of this letter from Maman had once again made his heart feel heavy and full of pain—a pain that he couldn't push away or think away or act away, no matter how hard he tried.

He stared down at the letter, wondering if he should even open it. Maybe whatever Maman had written would make him feel even worse! But finally, the urge became too strong. He pried the flap of the envelope open, pulled out the letter, unfolded it, and began to read. Maman wrote that she was doing well. She said she was still in Kronberg waiting to hear news about Papa. She asked how Henry was and said that she hoped he and Helen were taking care of one another. But as he reached the end of the letter, his grip on the paper tightened and he felt the blood rush up to his ears, pounding so hard he could hear nothing else.

I am sitting here remembering a time when the four of us went to the zoo back at home. Do you remember that day, my sweet boy? You were only five years old at the time. You wanted to see the lions more than any other animal. When we approached the lion cage, there was one enormous lion pacing back and forth at the front. You marched right up to the bars and tried to put your hand inside. Your Papa and I had to hold you back. You insisted that the lion didn't scare you. You were fearless.

I know there are times now when you must be feeling afraid. Even though Helen is there to help you, I know you must worry about me and about your Papa. But I want you to always remember that brave little boy who stood in front of the lion cage and believed he could tame even the wildest beast. You are that little boy! I love you always and hold you in my heart.

The letter jogged the distant memory for Henry— that day at the zoo, the sun so bright in the sky, Maman and Papa smiling. And it reminded him of the skit the clown had performed on that first visit to the convent, when he had pretended to be a lion tamer. Maybe that was part of what had inspired Henry in the first place, the memory of his own urge to be brave that day at the zoo. But that feeling was gone. Henry barely noticed the tears that had begun to stream down his cheeks. When he finished reading, he lowered his head onto his pillow and cried, long and hard. He didn't want to stop crying until he had cried every tear out of his body. Instead of making him feel better, the letter and the memory of that time had made him feel worse. It had opened a vault of feelings that he had tried to push away or keep so tightly bottled up that they didn't overwhelm him. Everything that the clown had taught him about being confident and strong suddenly evaporated like drops of water on a hot, sunny day. He didn't feel like a brave lion tamer at all, he thought. He felt as scared as the tiniest mouse.

CHAPTER 20

Henry

The day started like any other day. The morning bell woke him; he dressed and went for breakfast. Then Henry returned to his room to grab a few minutes of writing in his code book. He didn't always have time to do this. Chores or classes or some other activity often pulled him away. But this morning, he wanted to draw pictures of his mother and father. After getting the letter from Maman, he had been feeling gloomier than ever. It was so hard to push away those sad feelings once they swept over him. Even the clown, on his last visit to the convent, had noticed how down Henry was.

"We all have bad days, *mon petit muet*," the clown had said. "Don't be too hard on yourself."

But Henry hated the sad feelings. He knew drawing would help. He shaded in Papa's mustache and carefully drew his round glasses. He was just beginning to outline Maman's face when the bells began to chime, announcing that it was time to go for exercises.

Henry ignored the ringing. He needed to get the look on Maman's face just right, and for that, he needed more time. But then Paul, the boy Henry had fought with weeks earlier, came into their room. There was an uneasy truce between the two boys. They stayed out of each other's way, which worked fine.

Paul looked surprised to see Henry there. "You better get downstairs for exercises, or you're going to be in trouble." Paul pulled off the sweater he was wearing, threw it on his bed, and ran for the door before turning back to look at Henry. "Okay, don't say I didn't warn you." With that, he bolted from the room.

Henry continued drawing, but Paul's warning nagged at him. He knew Paul was doing him a favor. He would get in trouble if he didn't show up.

Henry sighed. Reluctantly, he dropped his code book on the bed. Then he ran out the door and raced down the stairs into the courtyard.

Twice a week, the nuns marched the children outside to run around the yard and do squats and sit-ups. The exercises were usually led by mean Sister Agnes. She always started off by saying things like, "Strong bodies make strong minds" or "Moving slowly will get you nowhere."

Henry didn't mind the exercises, not like some of the other boys in his dorm room who moaned and complained and dragged their feet. He liked running and working his muscles. He didn't even mind when Sister Agnes yelled at them to pick up the pace. He could run fast. He usually passed Helen, who jogged as slowly as a turtle while she talked to her friend Michelle. Helen could only talk to her friend when Sister Agnes wasn't looking. Otherwise, the mean nun would also shout things like, "Less talking or I will keep you out here all day." That would make everyone groan even more!

There were clouds overhead and the sky was dark. Everyone was waiting for the rain to come. A lot of the boys in his dorm were probably hoping the rain would come fast, so that they wouldn't have to exercise any more. But Henry didn't even mind the gray day. It matched his mood. Maybe running would help lift his spirits, he thought. Maybe the harder he ran, the less he would think about Maman, and home, and how hard it was to be left here. And maybe, if he ran really fast, he'd finish all his laps ahead of the others and he'd still have time to go back to his room and finish the drawings of Maman and Papa. It was worth a try.

He was on his tenth lap, and his neck and back were feeling sweaty. He reached up to wipe his forehead when Mère Supérieure came running toward them. Henry had never seen the head nun run before, and it was almost funny to watch her long black robe flowing behind her and her feet tripping over the uneven grass. But his heart froze a second later when he heard her yell, "Nazis are at the gate. Inside! Everyone inside!"

He came to a dead stop, along with all the children around him, like statues that had been placed in the yard. And then Mère Supérieure called a second time, "Inside, now!" And that was all it took for all the children to head for the doors of the convent. This time, *everyone* was running as fast as they could.

"Form lines! Remain calm," Sister Agnes shouted. But her face looked anything but calm. She was as white as the sheet on Henry's bed and breathing hard, as if she was the one who had done all the exercises.

"Follow Sister Agnes into the great hall!" Mère Supérieure instructed, standing by the door to help usher the children inside.

Henry ran up behind Helen, who had reached the door and stopped beside Mère Supérieure.

"Why are the Nazis here?" Henry heard her ask. He hadn't seen his sister look this scared since that day in town.

"They've asked to search your rooms," she said. Even Mère Supérieure's face was white.

"What are they searching for?" Helen asked the question that was pounding in Henry's mind.

Mère Supérieure shook her head. "We don't know. It's never happened before. But no need to worry." She said this last part loudly, so that all the children passing by could hear. "Just remain strong. And remember who you are."

Helen and Henry followed the last of the children into the convent, followed finally by Mère Supérieure. "Everyone to the great hall," she called. "Move quickly but in an orderly manner. We will wait there for instructions."

Helen turned and Henry locked eyes with hers, just as the skies outside opened up and the rain began to fall in fat drops. *Don't forget what happened in the store*, his stare said. He had to rely on Helen to remember their new names if the Nazis started asking questions. He knew he wouldn't be able to speak if they questioned him. Helen nodded and turned away, quickening her pace to catch up with the others as Henry felt a wave of relief sweep over him.

But a moment later, he remembered something, something that scared him enough to make his teeth chatter: his code book! In his rush to leave his dorm room and get to the courtyard for exercises, he had left the book uncovered on his bed. In it, he had written his real name. He had written about what he missed in Frankfurt and about his life before being left here. He had drawn that Star of David. Everything in that book pointed to him being a Jewish boy who was hiding here in the convent. If the Nazi soldiers searched the dorm rooms, they were bound to find it. They were bound to find him! And if they found out about him, then it wouldn't take much for them to find out about Helen and all the other children hiding here. That code book, which had helped him so much in the weeks since being here, was the thing that could now ruin everything.

There was only one thing to do.

The nuns were leading all the children toward the great hall, telling them to stay in line, stay calm, and move forward. Henry needed to get to his room, retrieve the book, and find a safer place to hide it. He had to think of a way to do that, and think fast! And then he saw his chance.

The group rounded a corner and was about to

walk by a closet that was usually used to store mops and pails to clean the convent floors. The door to the closet was usually shut tight. Today, it was wide open. Maybe the Nazis had already searched in there, Henry thought. Whatever the reason, he knew this was his one and only opportunity to get out of the line that was getting closer and closer to the great hall.

He didn't look around and didn't notice if anyone saw him. As he passed by the closet, he leapt from the line and dove in, pressing himself into the back corner. The children's footsteps disappeared. So far, his plan seemed to be working. But Henry knew that he wasn't in the clear yet.

His mouth was dry; his heart was pounding loud and hard. Along with the fear of being discovered in the mop closet, Henry was also terrified someone would notice that he wasn't with the others in the great hall. He already imagined Helen looking around and seeing that he wasn't there. He knew how much that would scare her. But he also knew he had to push away all those thoughts along with his own fear, and *move*. He could hear that the drizzle outside had turned into a downpour. Rain was pounding on the roof of the convent like a thousand horses' hooves. Taking a deep breath, Henry poked his head from the closet. No one was around. And a second later, he bolted up the stairs, taking the steps two at a time and glancing over his shoulder all the while. The coast was still clear.

He ran the length of the hallway and ducked into his room. He had no idea how much time he had before the soldiers would make their way upstairs to begin searching through the dorms. Rain was hammering against the window as he made a beeline for his bed and grabbed his code book, hugging it to his chest, all the while listening for footsteps signaling the approaching Nazis. And that was when the biggest problem of all came crashing down on him. Where could he possibly hide his book? Where would it be safe? There was no secret cave or locked safe to throw the book into. Under the bed? Out the window? They were all terrible ideas.

Then, above the sound of the rain, he heard footsteps in the hallway. Still holding tightly on to his code book, he turned to face the door.

A second later, Helen walked into his room.

CHAPTER 21

Helen

Helen had lost track of her brother in the commotion of following everyone back into the convent. She had thought Henry was behind her, assumed he had followed the crowd back inside and was lining up in the great hall, just as Mère Supérieure had instructed. But when Helen entered the hall and looked around, she was terrified to find that Henry was nowhere to be seen.

The noise level in the hall was rising along with the sense of confusion and fear. Helen could see it on everyone's faces. Many of the younger children were crying. Older ones were holding on to their hands.

But the older boys and girls looked just as terrified as the little ones. The nuns walked among the children, giving orders and trying their best to control the chaos.

"Remain calm." "Keep your voices down." "No need to be afraid." The nuns' instructions rose above the racket. But it didn't help that they themselves looked so afraid. The clamor would subside for a few seconds and then pick up again.

Helen's heart hammered in her chest. She was terrified at the thought of facing Nazi soldiers again. But first, she had Henry to worry about. The soldiers had not yet entered the hall. *They must be searching somewhere in the building*, Helen imagined. She had to find her brother before they appeared and began questioning everyone. Was he hiding out in some corner of the convent? Did he not realize how dangerous this was for him and for everyone else?

Helen's mind raced as her eyes darted around the room. The nuns were on the other side, surrounding the younger children and trying to help calm them. No one was looking her way. Pushing aside her own fears, Helen slipped out of the great hall. And in that same moment, she caught a glimpse of Henry running out of the mop closet and bolting up the staircase.

She followed, all the while looking over her shoulder to see if the nuns, or worse yet, the soldiers, were following her. So far, no one was around. She could hear the nuns still trying to calm the children. Up the stairs she crept and then walked the length of the hallway, her footsteps keeping beat with the rain pounding on the convent roof.

She expected to find Henry cowering under his bed or sitting in a corner of his room or buried under his covers. What she never expected was to see him standing in the middle of his dorm room clutching a notebook up against his chest so tightly that his knuckles were white. Even though she had never seen it up close, she knew immediately that it was the book Henry wrote in—the one he would hide away whenever she entered his room. Henry's body was rigid and his face streaked with fear.

"It's okay, Henry," she began, trying to keep her voice even as she approached him. "Just put the book away and come down to the hall." She reached out to place a hand on her brother's shoulder, but he shook her off. "I know the soldiers scare you"—she tried again—"they scare me, too. But we need to be downstairs with everyone else." She had to get Henry out of the dorm room. Now was not the time to be writing in this book of his.

But instead of putting the book back under his covers, Henry held it out to her.

Helen was taken aback. "You want me to look at this?"

He nodded, his eyes wide with fright.

"You want me to look *now*?" There was no time for this. They had to get back downstairs before someone noticed their absence. But Henry pushed the book into her hands and pleaded with his eyes for her to look inside.

And then, Henry opened his mouth and spoke.

"You have to help me," he said.

She had not heard Henry's voice in weeks, and even though it sounded raspy and weak, a wave of relief washed over Helen. Her arms fell loose and a brief smile stretched across her face. Henry was talking! But a moment later, her body tightened and her face fell as another thought came crashing down on her. Henry must be in desperate trouble to choose this moment to begin to talk. Helen took the book from him and opened it. She gasped out loud when she looked at the first page. There was Henry's real name, printed in big block letters, crossed out, and then written again. Beside the name was a small Star of David that Henry must have drawn. Flipping quickly through the pages, Helen read the list of things that he missed from home and the things he wanted to do when he returned to Frankfurt. On one of the pages, he had written, *We got into trouble at a store. I helped Helen when she almost said my name— my real name. I miss you, Maman. I miss you, Papa.*

Her heart began to pound uncontrollably once more. This was all the evidence the Nazi soldiers would need to expose Henry and perhaps all of the others at the convent as Jewish children in hiding. She looked up at her brother, and then back down at the book, desperately trying to come up with a plan.

"What are we going to do?" Henry asked.

It was still so strange to hear his voice, but Helen needed to focus and figure out their next move.

"We need to find a place to hide this—somewhere that isn't here in your room."

"I know," Henry replied. "Where?"

Helen's mind was racing. The mop closet downstairs? The pantry? The courtyard? The garden? She quickly ran through all those possibilities, not sure which might be a safe hiding place and not knowing how they would get to any of them. "I don't know, Henry, but we have to get out of here before someone finds us."

With no plan in mind, Helen grabbed Henry's arm, and together, they ran for the door. As they headed out into the hallway, they nearly plowed headlong into Albert.

"What are the two of you doing up here?" he whispered, glancing behind him. "I came to look for you when I saw that you weren't downstairs." Albert's face was flushed.

"We need to hide my code book," Henry replied, pointing to the notebook that Helen held tightly underneath her arm.

Albert's eyes widened as he looked at Henry and then glanced at Helen.

"I know," she replied. Albert looked as startled to hear Henry's voice as she had been. "We don't have much time." She quickly opened the notebook and showed it to Albert.

He took one look and shook his head, whistling softly under his breath. "This is bad," he said.

"We've got to find a place to put it," Helen said. "Somewhere the soldiers won't search."

She and Henry both looked at Albert, eyes pleading for help. Finally, he nodded.

"Okay, give it to me."

"What are you going to do?" Henry asked.

Albert lifted his shirt and placed the notebook against his chest. Then he lowered his shirt and tucked the ends securely into his trousers. "One step at a time. We need to get downstairs. Once we're in the hall with the others, I'll figure out what to do with this."

It wasn't a great plan, Helen reasoned. And it would put Albert in greater danger if the soldiers stopped him. But Helen had nothing more to offer. And Albert was right: the most important thing for now was to rejoin the others. Perhaps they could lose themselves in the crowd of children assembled downstairs and avoid the soldiers. With any luck, the Nazis would search the rooms and not the children themselves. She grabbed Henry's arm once more and followed Albert down the hallway. They were just beginning to head downstairs when a loud cry from down below brought the three of them to an abrupt stop.

CHAPTER 22

Helen

Someone was screaming, and it wasn't one of the other children. This was the voice of a grown-up. Then other voices joined in; Helen thought she could hear Mère Supérieure and even Sister Agnes shouting, "No! No! No!" Each cry grew louder than the one before. The sounds were coming from the great hall.

Helen locked eyes with Albert and Henry. Albert instinctively reached up to touch the front of his shirt. *What to do now?* Helen looked over her shoulder, wondering if they should retreat upstairs.

"We can't go back up." Albert was reading her

mind. Another cry echoed up the staircase. Helen thought it sounded like Sister Cecile.

"What's happening?" she whispered.

Henry moved closer to her. Albert shook his head. "I have no idea. But we've got to try and sneak back in."

Albert led the way, with Helen and Henry following close behind. The cries grew louder as they approached the door to the great hall. Helen could still not make out what was happening. Between the pounding in her chest and the rain on the convent roof, the sounds up ahead were muffled and hollow, as if she were standing in an empty drum, listening to noises echo around her. Henry winced. She realized she was clutching his arm so hard, she was hurting him. She softened her grip.

They kept their heads low as they crept into the back of the great hall. But no heads turned back to note their arrival. All eyes were focused on what was happening at the front of the room. Helen stretched her neck above and around the other children, who had gone silent, staring straight ahead of them, frozen and completely mesmerized by something. *But what?* And then she saw it. There at the front stood Sister Cecile. She was flanked on either side by two Nazi soldiers, each one holding her arms in a tight grip. Her head was down, her body crumpling

forward. The sharp screams Helen had heard moments earlier were coming from Sister Cecile. She
moaned and cried and gasped for air. Mère Supérieure
and Sister Agnes and all the other nuns stood close
by, their faces ghostly white. And then, another Nazi
soldier stepped forward—a terrifying and familiar
face! He was the same one who had confronted her
and Henry in the store weeks earlier. Henry sucked in
his breath and then clapped his hand over his mouth.
The soldier began talking to Mère Supérieure.

"Did you realize that you have a Jew hiding here
in the convent?"

Helen was confused. There were dozens of Jewish
children hiding here. But that wasn't what he was
talking about, she realized. As he spoke, he was pointing at Sister Cecile!

Helen's mind was racing a mile a minute. Sister
Cecile? Kind Sister Cecile? Was it possible that she
wasn't a nun? That she was also Jewish? That she
was hiding here, just like all the children? The Nazi
soldier was still talking.

"Someone spotted her in town. They recognized
her from somewhere else."

"We ... I ... we didn't—" Mère Supérieure stammered a reply.

"We'll take over from here, Sister," the soldier

continued. "No need to search the rooms for now. We're rooting out Jews who are hiding all over the countryside. But they won't stay hidden for long. We'll find them, and when we do …"

He didn't finish the sentence. He motioned for the other soldiers to take Sister Cecile away. They marched her—her head still down and moaning softly—through the great hall and past the children who watched in silent disbelief with mouths open, stepping aside to clear a path for the nun and her captors.

Helen still stood at the back of the hall, and still held on to Henry. Sister Cecile raised her head as she passed Helen. The nun who had been so kind to her from the moment she had arrived here met Helen's eyes with her own. And then she lowered her head once more and was led from the room. The Nazi soldier who had stopped them in town paused in front of Helen.

"Ah, it's the young girl and her shy brother. We meet again," the soldier said. Then he leaned forward and added, "I told you the Jews were everywhere." He stood back up and peered at them. "What did you say your names were?"

Helen couldn't breathe. It felt as if there was a rope around her neck, getting tighter and tighter.

She opened her mouth, struggled for air. And then Henry stepped forward.

"I'm Andre. And this is my sister, Claire." He said this clearly, almost defiantly.

The soldier laughed. "So, the shy one has a voice after all," he said. And then he continued out the door.

CHAPTER 23

Helen

In the days since the Nazis had come and taken away Sister Cecile, everyone walked around the convent in silence. The children looked afraid and uncertain. And the nuns looked dazed. Mère Supérieure had said that a search like this had never happened before. *Why now?* Helen wondered. Would the soldiers be back? And next time, would they come looking for the children?

"Did you have any idea about Sister Cecile?" Michelle asked, as she and Helen sat in the dining hall following lunch. They couldn't seem to get up from the table; a kind of despair was weighing over them like a heavy coat. It was hard to move. It was hard to do anything.

"Not really," Helen said. But there had been signs, she realized, things about Sister Cecile that Helen had ignored or skirted past with hardly a second thought. There was her deep empathy, as if she really understood what it was like for Helen and the others to have been left here; her desire to reach out to the children as they adjusted to life at the convent; even her reluctance to confront Sister Agnes after Helen had spoken to her about the nun's constant punishments. From the start, Sister Cecile had been different from all the other nuns. *She was one of us. All along, she was one of us.*

As she shared these thoughts with Michelle, something else occurred to her. "I wonder if Cecile is even her real name."

"You're right!" Michelle sat upright, eyes wide. "I'm sure she changed it just like the rest of us. We have no idea who she really was."

Helen slumped forward and lowered her head on her hand. "Can you imagine how alone she must have felt? I mean, at least we get to talk to each other. Sister Cecile ... or whoever she is ... had no one."

"Where do you think they've taken her?"

Helen squeezed her eyes shut. "I don't want to think about it. It scares me too much."

The girls sat in silence. As much as she wanted to push the thoughts away, terrible images bombarded Helen's mind, like a persistent ghost hovering above her head. Maman and others had spoken of prisons where Jews were being tortured and killed. Is that where Sister Cecile had been taken? Is that where Papa was?

"I have a headache. I need to get some air." Helen pushed her chair back from the table and stood. "Will you let Sister Agnes know that I've gone to the infirmary?" She paused. "Have you noticed the change in Sister Agnes?" she asked.

The punishments from Sister Agnes had stopped completely in the days following the search of the convent. The nun who had always looked sour and stern had become quiet and almost meek. The other morning, Sister Agnes had passed Helen on her way to the dining hall. There had been a button missing from the top of her blouse and her hair had been messy and falling in her eyes; she had not slept well in days—another leftover from the search. Sister Agnes had stopped her at the bottom of the staircase and looked Helen up and down. The nun's eyes had zoomed in on Helen's hair and missing button. Normally, there would have been a long lecture on obeying the rules and being grateful for the generosity of the nuns. And then she would have told Helen to do the dishes or mop the floors. But not this time. This time, the nun who always yelled hadn't raise her voice at all. She had just told Helen to go back to her room and clean herself up. She had even patted her on the arm!

"I've wanted her to stop picking on me since the day I arrived here," Helen said. "And now that she has, I almost wish she'd start again."

On the way out of the dining hall, Helen bumped into Albert. Although they had talked briefly since the search, she hadn't had a chance to thank him properly for everything he'd done to help with Henry's code book. To be honest, it was hard for her to find the words to express how grateful she felt. If it hadn't been for Albert, she wasn't sure what she would have done. She told Albert all of this and his face reddened.

"I didn't really know what to do with the book either," Albert replied. "Sticking it under my shirt wasn't a very good plan. But it was the only one I had. We were just lucky that the Nazis didn't search us."

"What do you think is going to happen now?"

"I've heard that Mère Supérieure wants to meet with all of us. There's something going on—I'm not sure what. But I think the Nazis may come back. We're not out of the woods."

Helen's stomach was sinking faster and deeper than she had imagined was possible. It didn't surprise her to hear Albert say this. She knew in her heart that things were escalating and not in a good way: first, the confrontation in town, and now, the search of the convent. The dangers out there felt as if they were drawing nearer and nearer.

"I gave Henry back his code book," Albert added. "But it's not safe with him. We're going to have to do something about that."

CHAPTER 24

Helen

Just as Albert had said, all the children were asked to meet with Mère Supérieure, one by one. Helen was summoned just after breakfast the next day. When she arrived at Mère Supérieure's office, Marcel was just coming out.

"Marcel!" she exclaimed, as he shut the door behind him. She hadn't seen him in such a long time, not since before the raid by the Nazi soldiers. "Are you here to give us a show?" Everyone was in desperate need of something to take their minds off of recent events.

Marcel shook his head. "I'm afraid not. I know

this has been a tough time for everyone. But I hear that your brother has begun to talk," he said with a smile. "That's good news."

Helen nodded. "Everyone kept telling me it would take time for him to adjust. But I don't think that had anything to do with him talking. He needed my help and had to ask for it." She didn't tell Marcel about Henry's code book.

"Your brother is strong," he replied. "And you are, too. Don't forget that."

Just then, the door to Mère Supérieure's office opened. The head nun stood on the other side. "Claire," she said. "Please come in."

Helen gulped, said good-bye to Marcel, and entered. Once Helen was seated in front of her, Mère Supérieure wasted no time.

"We've been having many discussions—the other sisters and I—since ... since ... since ..." She hesitated, as if she couldn't even say the words *Sister Cecile's arrest*. Finally, she breathed out what sounded like a painful sigh. "At any rate, the protection of all the children here at the convent is our most important concern. And I'm afraid we may no longer be able to keep you safe."

"Did you know?" Helen asked hesitantly. "Did you know about Sister Cecile?"

Mère Supérieure looked away and then back at Helen. "Of course," she replied. "But I was the only one. The other sisters knew nothing." Mère Supérieure looked away again, her voice sounding wistful. "She played her part so beautifully—Sister Cecile. I really thought we were in the clear." Then she coughed, clearing her throat. "I'm afraid it's only a matter of time before the Nazis put two and two together—before they realize that the rest of you …" She didn't finish that sentence.

Helen lowered her head. Lately, all anyone talked about was how dangerous everything was: dangerous to be here, dangerous to be out there, dangerous to talk to anyone, dangerous to be Jewish. She was so sick of it all. Why were people so hateful and intent on hurting her and others like her? Why couldn't everything just go back to the way it had been before all these troubles began? She could feel angry tears stinging her eyes and blinked them away.

"I'm making arrangements to move you and all of the children."

Helen lifted her head. "Move us where?"

"Switzerland," Mère Supérieure replied. "It's safer than Germany or Austria, or even France."

Helen gulped. Her first thought, as always, was about her mother. How would Maman ever be able to find her if she and Henry were moved away? But it was the first time she had heard any mention of that small country to the east.

"Switzerland has resisted Adolf Hitler as much as it can," Mère Supérieure continued. "For now."

For now? "What do you mean that you're going to move us there?" Helen asked.

"There are some people who will help get you to the border—hiking through the forest and across the hills that separate us from Switzerland."

It reminded Helen of the journey they had made from Kronberg to the convent here in France. She hadn't imagined that she would be on the run again.

"You'll be leaving in groups—three or four of you at a time."

"Why such a small group?" Helen asked. If they needed to leave, then perhaps they should all leave together!

"This journey won't be easy. And a small group is less likely to be detected in the forest. I'm trying to put groups together who will work well with each other—help each other along the way."

There were so many questions running through Helen's mind. Who were these people who would take them to the border? What would this difficult journey really be like? How long would they be traveling? When would they leave? Mère Supérieure held up her hand as if she anticipated the barrage of questions.

"There are still many details to be worked out. As soon as everything is in place, I'll let you know when it's your time to go."

A sudden, horrifying thought stabbed at Helen. "Excuse me, Mère Supérieure, but what about my brother? Am I going without him?"

For a moment, the head nun looked startled. "Oh my goodness, no. Of course he'll go with you. I would never think of separating the two of you. I had hoped that you would explain all of this to him. I think he'll accept it better coming from you rather than me. I know he's had a more difficult time being here."

In the chaos following the raid on the convent, Helen didn't even know if Mère Supérieure realized that Henry was talking again. She appeared to be so preoccupied with other things.

Mère Supérieure unfolded herself from her chair and came around to stand in front of Helen. "Everything you need to know will be explained to you in due time. I just want you to be prepared."

Helen felt hot tears gather behind her eyes, and she blinked furiously. "My parents?"

Mère Supérieure leaned down to take Helen's hands in hers. "I will try to get word to your mother," she said.

Was there a chance that her mother might arrive to rescue her and Henry before they were sent away?

For a second, Helen had that fleeting and desperate thought. But a moment later, Mère Supérieure added, "But I can't promise."

Helen nodded as the tears finally began to stream down her cheeks. She glanced up at the painting of Jesus. Then, releasing Mère Supérieure's hands, she stood and ran from the office.

Chapter 25

Henry

Henry was writing in his code book again. When Albert had given it back to him after the raid, he had grabbed it gratefully and clutched it to his chest. It was like being reunited with his best friend. Now, Henry was making a list of the things he wanted to do when all the troubles were over and he could finally leave the convent:

1. *Ride my bicycle.*
2. *Walk to school.*
3. *Eat pudding.*

Henry paused and looked down at the page. His

favorite flavor was chocolate. Papa liked vanilla, but Helen and Maman were also chocolate lovers. Maman would cook up a big batch of chocolate pudding, letting it bubble on the stove until it was thick. Then it had to cool down before she would let him have some. The waiting was the hardest part. But Maman would let him lick the pot, and she didn't even care when his mouth and nose were covered in a ring of chocolate gooeyness.

Henry flipped back through the pages of his code book, pausing to stare at the Star of David that he had drawn on the first page, and at the words *safe* and *harbor.* After those soldiers had come through the convent and taken kind Sister Cecile, he felt less safe than ever. And he was missing his parents more and more. And on top of that, the clown hadn't come to perform in such a long time.

Something was happening at the convent. The nuns huddled in groups, whispering, and he knew that some of the children were being called in to meet with Mère Supérieure. He didn't know what that was all about. But it couldn't be good. He sighed deeply and turned to a clean page in his book. Just then, the door to his room creaked open. It was Helen. She paused behind it, asking, "Can I come in?"

Normally, Henry would have shut his code book tightly and shoved it quickly under his blanket as he had always done. But there was no point in hiding it from her now.

Without waiting for a reply, Helen opened the door and walked into Henry's room. Albert was right behind her. They sat down on his bed, one on either side of him. Helen had that look on her face—not as bad as the look she had had when they were in the store and the Nazi soldiers had come up to him, and not as bad as the look she'd had when the convent was raided, but still pretty serious.

"Is everything okay?" Henry asked. His voice still sounded a bit hoarse, not a surprise since he hadn't used it in so long.

"We're going to be leaving the convent, Henry," Helen said. "A bunch of us have already met with Mère Supérieure. She's making arrangements to send us to Switzerland. Do you know where that is?"

Of course, he had heard of the country, but he didn't know much about it. "Why?" he asked.

"She says it isn't safe here anymore."

"Is it because the soldiers came here and took Sister Cecile away?"

Helen nodded. "Yes—that, and seeing the Nazis in town. She says that Switzerland is a better place for us right now. I'm not exactly sure how we're going to get there, and I don't know when we're going to leave. But it's probably going to be soon." She went on to explain that they would be traveling in small groups and that the hike from southern France to Switzerland would be hard, but they would be together. He was glad to hear that last part.

"No one knows much more than that," Albert continued. "But there's something else that we came to talk to you about."

Henry knew what Albert was going to say and jumped in before the words were out of his mouth.

"It's my book, isn't it?"

This was the other thing Henry had been dreading since the terrible raid—the panic he had felt thinking the soldiers might find the book; how he had not known what to do with it or where to hide it; how Albert had shoved it under his shirt. Henry winced as those images flashed through his mind again.

"It's just too dangerous to keep it here if the soldiers come back to search again," Helen said.

"But if we're leaving, then maybe I can take it with me." Henry couldn't bear the thought of giving it up.

"I don't know how much we'll be able to take with us when we go," Helen replied. "But I don't think it will be a good idea to take that book along."

"But why?"

Helen pointed out the window. "What if we run into somebody out there? It's too dangerous to have something like this with you."

Henry understood what that meant. The thought of being stopped by Nazi soldiers while they were on the run was also terrifying. "I don't want to rip it up," Henry said sadly. It would be terrible to do that to the writing that meant so much to him.

"That's what we've come to talk to you about," Albert said. "We have a better idea. We think you should bury it in the courtyard."

Henry looked at him.

"I told Sister Agnes that I would work in the garden tomorrow," Helen said. "You'll come with me and we'll dig a hole and put your notebook in the ground. That way, you won't have to destroy it."

Bury it in the ground? It was a good idea—and maybe the only idea. Burying his code book would keep it safe and whole, even if it wasn't with him.

After Helen and Albert left him, Henry opened his code book one last time. On a fresh page, he printed his real name in big letters. Underneath it, he wrote, *We are leaving.*

The next day, clutching the code book to his chest, Henry left his dorm room and joined Helen and Albert in the courtyard.

"Bring your book over to that flower bed," Helen said, pointing to a bright corner of the garden. "The earth is softer there and you can dig a deep hole."

Henry walked to the flower bed and chose a spot

between patches of red and yellow flowers. He fell to his knees and began to dig, pulling up mounds of soil with his hands and piling them to one side, over and over until he had created a hill of dirt next to a hole in the ground that was as deep as the length of his arm, and just as wide. He didn't want Albert or Helen to help him. He had to do this on his own. Finally, he took his code book in his hands and stared at it one last time. Then he gently placed it in the ground, covering it with the dirt he had set aside. He patted the mound with both hands before standing up.

The flowers on either side of the mound looked nice, and their smell reminded him of the perfume Maman used to wear.

Helen walked up to stand next to him. "You'll make other books in the future, Henry."

"And it'll be here for you if you ever come back to this place," added Albert.

Henry looked up at the convent walls. He didn't know if he'd ever be back here and he wasn't sure he wanted to return. Besides, he had found his voice again, and he knew that he didn't need the writing, at least for now.

Finally, he wiped his hands on his trousers, looked up at Helen, and said, "I'm ready to go."

CHAPTER 26

Helen

Helen knelt in the chapel, staring up at the statue of Jesus Christ as the church service neared completion. Normally, Helen went through the motions of praying without feeling anything inside of her. She always reminded herself that she was Jewish and this was not her house of worship. This was all just pretend, a way of surviving—it didn't mean anything more to her. But not lately. Lately, the church services had become more of a refuge for Helen—a place where she could close her eyes and have a real conversation with God.

She reached into her pocket and pulled out two

photographs, glancing around to make sure no one was watching her. Then, she smoothed them out and held them in front of her. They were pictures of her mother and father. Maman had included them in the letter she had sent to Helen. She had returned her letter to Mère Supérieure just as she'd been instructed. But she had kept these photographs, telling no one about them, not even Albert or Michelle. She touched the faces of her parents, first one and then the other, running her finger across their eyes, noses, and down to their mouths. Where were they? she wondered for what felt like the millionth time. When would she see them again? With the pictures clasped tightly in her hands, she turned her eyes toward the front of the chapel.

It's me, Helen, she whispered softly. *I'm going to use my real name so that you know who's talking to you, even though everyone around here keeps calling me by that other name.* She took a breath. *Please make sure Papa is okay, and please try to have Maman come back to get us.* She paused and glanced down at her photographs again, thinking about the next part of her prayer before continuing. *The nuns are going to send us away from here. They say it's to a safer place. There's probably nothing you can do about it.* She took another deep breath. *But maybe if you could just look after us—especially Henry. Just please try to keep us safe.*

Then, for good measure, she whispered a Hebrew prayer. It was one that Papa had always recited aloud over her and Henry on the Sabbath, and it began with the words *May God bless you and watch over you.* She figured it would also be good for her parents. Finally, she slipped the photographs back into her pocket, crossed herself as she had been taught, and stood up as the service came to an end. Mère Supérieure stopped her as she left the chapel.

"It's time," the head nun said.

So soon! Helen gulped and nodded. It's not that she wasn't expecting this. Several children had already left the convent, disappearing in the middle of the night. Their empty beds in the morning were a stark reminder that her day was coming. Still, hearing those words coming out of Mère Supérieure's mouth made Helen's head spin. She reached out to one of the pews to steady herself.

"After dinner this evening, you and Henry must pack a few articles of clothing into a backpack that you'll be given," Mère Supérieure said. "Take only those items that are essential. Then come to the dining hall. You'll leave after dark."

Helen still had so many questions. How long would they be traveling for? In what direction? How difficult would the journey be? And perhaps most importantly, who would be taking them? But when she opened her mouth to ask, Mère Supérieure stopped her with a hand on her arm.

"Everything you need to know will be explained to you once you are on your way."

"Our mother?" Helen squeaked this out.

Mère Supérieure looked at her and then simply shook her head.

Helen knew it was a desperate wish that Maman might return for them before they had to leave. Now the clock had wound down, and no one was coming to their rescue.

Chapter 27

Helen

Helen went through the rest of her day in a daze, moving from chores to classes and then to meals. After dinner, she retreated to her dorm room to pack her things into the backpack that one of the nuns had given her. The other girls stared at her with expressions of compassion mixed with fear. Some gave her quick hugs, muttering words of support: "Good luck." "Everything will be okay." "We'll miss you." Some avoided her completely. Perhaps they could think of nothing to say that might help. Perhaps they wondered and worried when their own departure day would come.

It was just as well. She was so scared; she didn't really want to talk to anyone, for fear of breaking down. Maybe Henry had figured that out already, she thought. Perhaps at times, silence was better than talking.

But, of course, she couldn't hide any of her feelings from Michelle. Helen had avoided her friend for most of the day, unsure of how they would be able to say good-bye to one another. But now, it was Michelle who sat with her as she packed.

Michelle bit her lower lip. "I knew this was coming. But now, it's all happening so fast."

Michelle had also had her meeting with Mère Supérieure but was still waiting to hear about her departure day. "I wish I was coming with you," she added.

"Me, too. Mère Supérieure is keeping everything a secret for some reason."

"Switzerland!" Michelle shook her head. "Do you even know how you're going to get there?"

"I'm not sure. Mère Supérieure is keeping that a secret, too." She threw some underwear into the backpack. At that, Michelle stood up.

"Here," she said. "At least let me help you pack. You're making a mess of all your things."

Helen smiled and stepped back to let Michelle fill her backpack with the trousers, shirts, and socks that

Mère Supérieure had given her to pack for the journey. Helen didn't even know where the clothing had
come from. Finally, Michelle turned away to her own
storage cupboard. She pulled out the green ribbon
that she had gotten on her very last outing to town
and held it out to Helen. "You never got a special treat
when you went to town. You never got anything! So I
want you to have this. Maybe you'll think of me when
you wear it."

Helen took the ribbon and pressed it up to her
face. "I don't need anything to help me remember
you," she said. "But I'll keep this with me, always. I
don't know what I would have done here without
you," she added, feeling the tears gather behind her
eyes. Who would she talk to when Michelle wasn't
around? Who would be her friend out there?

"You'll be just fine," Michelle replied. Her voice
quivered and she struggled to keep it even. "You can
manage anything."

Helen wiped her eyes. "Just stay out of Sister
Agnes's way," she said. "You never know when she'll
go back to barking at everyone."

Michelle laughed softly. "I'll try!" She finished
packing Helen's bag and pulled the drawstring to tie
the opening together. Then she handed the backpack
to Helen.

"I don't want to say good-bye," Helen cried.

Michelle nodded. "Me neither."

"I have to believe that I'll see you again."

"Me, too."

Helen grabbed Michelle in a strong hug. "Just stay safe," she said as the two girls stood back and faced each other again. Then Helen took a deep breath. "Okay, I think I'm ready to go."

Before collecting Henry and heading down to the dining hall as instructed, Helen searched the halls for Albert. He was nowhere to be found, and Helen's spirits plummeted. How could she possibly leave without saying good-bye to her friend? But there was nothing she could do about it. They had to get to the dining hall as quickly as possible. Perhaps Mère Supérieure or one of the other nuns would say good-bye for her. It wasn't what she wanted, but it would have to do.

She went to get Henry, who stood ready in the doorway of his room, looking dwarfed by the backpack he carried. His face was more pale and downcast than she had seen in such a long time. Helen felt just as afraid as Henry looked. Her knees felt wobbly, and she clenched her hands together to try and stop them from shaking.

Mère Supérieure stood in the dining hall with Sister Agnes and all the other nuns—and Marcel! *What is he doing here?* Helen wondered. He certainly wasn't here to give a show this late at night! And why was he dressed in black from head to toe? Just then, he looked up and caught Helen's eye. He walked over to her.

"Tonight, I'm a guide," he said, pointing to the backpack that he was carrying. "*Un passeur.*"

Helen glanced over at Henry, whose face brightened immediately when he saw Marcel. But she was still puzzled.

"I thought you were a performer," she said.

Marcel chuckled. "I do many things," he replied. "But this is perhaps my most important work. I'm the one who's going to be taking you to the border. And I'll help you get across to safer territory. Switzerland hasn't fallen under Hitler's spell the way other countries have," he added.

"You're the one taking us?" The news was making Helen's head spin. She had only seen Marcel as one thing—an entertainer. Now suddenly, he had become something else—the person who was meant to save them.

"I've done this many times," he said, noting the confusion in Helen's eyes. "You'll be safe. I promise."

Helen wasn't sure he could make that kind of promise when everything was so unpredictable. What about the Nazis who patrolled in the forests of southern

France, looking for Jews? Could anyone protect her from them?

Just then, she felt a gentle tugging on her arm. She looked down and into Henry's eyes.

"I believe him, Helen," Henry said. "He can do anything." He looked up at Marcel. "Can't you?"

"It won't be easy," Marcel replied, choosing his words carefully. "But I'll be with you every step of the way. I won't let anything happen to you." He looked up. "And here's the third member of the group."

Just then, Albert walked into the dining room. Helen's first thought was that he was there to say good-bye to them. But no; he also carried a backpack.

"Are you coming, too?" she asked hopefully.

He smiled. "I am. I guess Mère Supérieure figured we would work well together."

"I'm so glad!" she said, realizing how much she had come to count on Albert. It was a huge relief to know that he was coming with them.

But she had no time to say anything more. Just then, Sister Agnes walked up to her. She squinted at Helen, running her eyes from the top of her head down to her shoes. Helen stiffened, wondering if the nun would reprimand her one last time for how she was dressed or how she had prepared for her departure.

But instead, Sister Agnes simply said, "I will be praying for you." And then, she lifted her hand and held it out to Helen, inviting her to take it.

"Thank you, Sister," Helen replied. She knew she wouldn't miss this nun, not the way that she would miss some of the others. She wouldn't miss Sister Agnes's daily scrutiny or the many punishments she had received at her hands. But Helen had come to realize that Sister Agnes did care, in her own unusual way. She had certainly shown that to be true during the terrible confrontation with the Nazi soldiers in town, and after that as well. Helen extended her own hand, accepting Sister Agnes's handshake as an honest moment of truce.

Marcel stood before the three children. "My lovely friends," he began. "We're going on an adventure tonight. There will be a lot of walking, and we'll have to keep silent most of the time. Will you be able to do that?"

All three of them nodded.

And then Marcel turned to Henry. "You already have some experience at this. So it should be simple, yes?"

Was that a small smile Helen saw pass over Henry's lips?

Marcel reached into his own backpack and pulled

out some papers. "These are your new documents. You'll carry them with you on our journey."

He handed a paper to Helen. It was an identity document with her picture on it. And the name on the paper, written in carefully scripted black ink, was Claire Rochette. Where had these papers come from? Helen looked up at Marcel. He caught her glance and smiled.

"Not only am I a wonderful mime artist and an excellent guide, I'm also a good forger, don't you think? No one will ever know that these documents are fakes."

Helen looked at the papers again. On the line beside the word *Religion* Marcel had printed *Catholic*. She wondered who might be inspecting her documents. But she pushed that thought aside for now, along with all the anxiety that came with it.

"I have to take a look inside your bags—just to make sure you're not bringing too much with you," Marcel continued. "The terrain will be difficult at times, and you'll need all your strength for the journey. I don't want you burdened by too many things."

She watched as Marcel quickly rummaged through Albert's bag and removed a couple of sweaters, placing them in a pile to one side. Then he nodded approvingly. He did the same with a few of Henry's things. But she knew what Marcel was going to find in her backpack even before he untied the strings and began to rifle through it. The photographs of her parents were there, hidden between the layers of her clothing, but easily discovered by Marcel, who pulled them out and stared down at them, and then up at Helen. She glanced over at Henry, who was staring at the photographs.

"They're just pictures," she began hoarsely. "I thought ..." And then she faltered.

Marcel shook his head. "I'm afraid we can't bring them. I know you understand."

Before Helen could say another word, Mère Supérieure stepped forward. She raised her hand and made the sign of the cross in the air above the heads of the three young people. "Go in safety, my children," she said. "And may God bless and watch over you."

There was no more time to think about her precious photographs. This was it! Helen placed her backpack over her shoulders, walked out of the dining hall, and followed her brother, Albert, and Marcel out the doors of the convent and into the warm night air.

CHAPTER 28

Henry

Henry lagged behind the others, thinking about the photographs of Maman and Papa. He hadn't known Helen had had those pictures—didn't know where she had gotten them. But when the clown had pulled them out of her backpack, he had almost cried out loud. He hadn't seen his parents' faces in so long. And now the pain of missing them was so big, it was wrapping around his heart and squeezing until he thought it might burst. He longed for them to come back. But now that he and Helen had left the convent, he was scared that he might never see Maman and Papa again. Henry shook his head. *No!* He couldn't let himself think like that. For now, he had to follow the others and keep walking.

He could see Helen looking back at him as they marched through the forest. And even though it was so dark he couldn't see her face, he imagined the look that was on it—one that he'd seen many times. She would be worried about him and wanting to do something to help. But there was nothing she could do to take away this sadness. At least the clown was there, leading them. There were so many things that Henry could worry about, but the one thing he felt sure of was that the clown would keep them safe. Henry pulled his shoulders back and picked up his pace, passing Helen and Albert until he was walking side by side with the clown.

The clown looked over at Henry when they were alongside each other and said, "I know you must be missing your parents, and I'm so sorry about that."

It was as if he was a mind reader. He understood Henry so much better than anyone else. "Why are you doing this?" Henry asked.

"Doing what?" The clown's pace did not slow as he and Henry talked.

"Helping children like us. It's so dangerous for you. You could be acting on a stage somewhere. You could be famous. Why are you doing this?"

The clown glanced over at Henry. "I haven't always

been Marcel Marceau—or 'the clown,' as you and the others call me," he said. "I once had a different last name."

"Was it changed the way the tall nun changed our names?" Henry asked.

"I changed it myself."

Why would anyone want to change their name? Henry wondered.

"I was Marcel Mangel, the son of a Jewish butcher," the clown continued. "But I decided to call myself Marceau after a famous French general who fought in this country years ago. Right now, I have no idea where my parents are," he added. "When the Nazis marched into eastern France, I went to join the partisans."

"The partisans?" Henry had no idea what that was.

"An underground movement," the clown said. "We think of ourselves as freedom fighters. In our own way, we're trying to fight back—holding rallies, demonstrations, getting information across the country, interrupting the progress of the Nazis. There are many people like me who are part of the Resistance, doing all of those things and more."

"So you decided to help children like me and Helen and Albert get across the border?"

The clown nodded. "I needed to find something important to do. Don't get me wrong, I love to perform.

But helping in this way has given me a sense of purpose." He glanced over at Henry. "Can you understand that?"

Henry nodded. "I think so. And your parents?"

"I'm hoping that they're safe."

"That's just like us," Henry exclaimed.

"We seem to have a lot in common, Henry."

Henry smiled. "You didn't call me *le muet*."

"I don't think that's your name anymore, is it?"

Henry thought about that for a moment. "No."

Then the clown smiled. "You stay close to me, my friend. You'll be my assistant and we'll lead the way for the others, won't we?"

Henry had no idea where they were going or how he could help get them there. But he felt his chest swell with pride. And for the moment, he forgot about his parents and all his other worries.

Deeper into the forest they trekked, staying well clear of the town, lit up in the distance—the town where the horrible Nazi soldiers had tried to question him. He looked away from those lights, looked straight ahead of him, placing one foot in front of the other, stepping over deep earthy ruts and tree roots that bulged from the ground. Leaves rustled softly above Henry's head. Every now and then, he caught a peek at stars that sparkled in the clear night sky. And then, they would disappear, swallowed up by the trees that towered above him. Small animals hid from view but called out to one another from branches and furrows; an owl hooted, a small fox growled, a rabbit darted away when they approached. It was so peaceful out here, Henry thought—too peaceful to be dangerous. At least, that's what he hoped.

At times, it felt as if they were walking in circles, first in one direction, and then turning around and going completely the opposite way, as if they were starting again. The forest would thin out, and then the trees would multiply and thicken and practically shove them off the path with their massive overgrowth. But the clown led the way as if he had walked this route dozens of times. Every now and then, he paused to check the sky and then sprinted forward again, barely looking behind him to see if the children were close.

Henry kept up with every step, feeling the muscles in his legs working harder than when he had run laps in the courtyard. Still, his breathing had become shallow and quick, and he could feel the sweat rolling down his back and dampening his shirt and the backpack that he carried.

Every once in a while, he looked over his shoulder at Helen. He didn't want her to fall too far behind. But Albert was right next to her, and so far, she was keeping up, though she was starting to look tired.

Suddenly, the clown raised his hand and came to an abrupt stop.

The children paused behind him, waiting and listening. But the only noise Henry could hear was the sound of their own breathing, each one gulping in air and trying to recover from the long and difficult night hike. Henry peered around the clown, who was still stopped on the path, his arm held straight up in the air. He could just make out a clearing up ahead and what looked like some small farmhouses. The clown suddenly turned and motioned for everyone to come closer. He bent down to whisper to them.

"It'll start to get light soon. We need to get out of the woods and find a place to rest. I know a farmer here who'll let us use his barn. He's a good man," he added. "Wait here and I'll go and talk to him." And with that, the clown disappeared, walking out of the forest and toward the lights of the farmhouse.

Henry sank down into the soft dirt. How long had they been walking? he wondered. Probably hours. His body longed for sleep. If he could, he would have closed his eyes right here in the woods and drifted off. But he willed himself to stay awake and alert. Helen and Albert lay on the ground close to him. Neither one was talking. Everyone seemed too exhausted to say a word.

A few minutes passed, and then Henry heard a rustling in the bushes ahead. The clown reappeared and motioned for the three of them to follow him. Henry pulled himself from the ground and crept after the clown, ducking down as they crossed the open field toward a barn that seemed impossibly far away. The forest had offered some comforting protection. Here in the open, he felt as if a thousand eyes were watching him. He picked up his pace.

When they finally reached the barn and went inside, the smell of fresh hay mixed with cow manure filled his nostrils. It was overpowering at first, nearly taking his breath away. He wrinkled his nose as he climbed after the clown up a steep ladder and into the hayloft. Helen and Albert were right behind him.

The clown motioned for each of them to find a place in the loft. Henry moved to a far corner. He brushed aside a spider web and let his body sink into the soft and prickly hay, repositioning himself several times until he had found a comfortable spot. He had no time to think about where they were or how far they still had to go. He had no chance to wonder where his parents were. He had no time to worry about Helen and whether or not she was okay. He was asleep as soon as his head settled onto the hay.

CHAPTER 29

Helen

The sun woke Helen, peeking through cracks in the barn roof above her hayloft bed. She blinked several times and stretched, uncertain at first about where she was. And then it all came into focus: the hours and hours they had walked before they had finally stopped to get some rest. Helen hadn't been sure how much longer she could have gone on. And all the while they'd been walking, she'd remembered that other escape, the one that had brought her and Henry to the convent. Maman had also made them trek for long distances. And while the paths had been smoother and easier to walk across, the worry about where they were heading had been equally intense.

It was quiet up here in the hayloft. The only sounds were some birds chirping in the distance and the cows down below, rustling in their stalls and snorting and mooing softly. She rolled over and looked around. Henry was still fast asleep. She could hear his soft snores coming from the far corner of the loft. Marcel had disappeared. But Albert was sitting up and looking at her.

She propped herself up on her elbow. "Good morning."

He smiled. "I think it's way past morning. How did you sleep?"

"Really well!" That was true. She had slept better than she had in weeks. The exhaustion after the long hike, mixed with the fresh night air, had worked magic on her. She had not stirred once after laying her head down in the loft.

"Me, too," Albert replied. "That's a first for me." Then he nodded toward Henry. "Your brother is still out like a light. How do you think he's doing?"

Helen pushed herself up to a sitting position and glanced again at Henry. "I'm not sure. I'm never really sure these days. He looked pretty upset when he saw those photographs of my parents."

"I'm sorry you couldn't bring them with you," Albert said.

Helen gulped. She was trying so hard not to wallow in her own sadness over losing the pictures of Maman and Papa. "It was stupid of me to think I could. As soon as Marcel said he was going to go through our backpacks, I knew he would find them." She closed her eyes, trying to capture in her mind the images of her parents, knowing that would have to hold her for the next while. Then she opened her eyes again and looked at Albert. "What time do you think it is?"

He crawled across the hay to press his face against the cracks in the barn board, squinting to get a look at the position of the sun in the sky. "I'm guessing it's mid-afternoon. Marcel said that we'd sleep during the day and move through the night."

Helen nodded. "Thanks for staying close to me out there." Albert had not left her side during their entire hike. Even when she had thought she might be faltering and lagging behind, Albert had slowed his pace to walk beside her.

"No problem," he replied, a sleepy grin on his face. "We have to stick together."

Just then, there was a rustling from down below and the sound of someone climbing the ladder. Helen froze instinctively, a slight chill passing over her body.

Marcel's face appeared at the top of the ladder and he grinned over at them. Then he slung a package onto the hay and climbed the rest of the way up to sit next to them in the loft.

Marcel opened the package as Henry began to stir. Inside were several fresh baguettes, some cheese wrapped in wax paper, and a few bright red tomatoes. He pulled out a jar of milk, which he set down on the straw. The smell of sweet yeasty bread filled the hayloft.

"As I said, the farmer is a good man," he said, as he pulled a knife from a holder in the back of his belt and began to cut up the cheese and tomatoes, dividing it among the children. "Eat as much as you can. I'm not sure when we're going to have this kind of feast again." As he said this, he tore off chunks of bread to pass around. Then he handed the jar of milk to Helen, motioning for her to take a swig before passing it on.

Helen drank the milk and gobbled her portion of food with hardly a breath between bites. The bread was still warm, and the cheese was soft and tart. The tomatoes were ripe and oozed juice that dribbled down her chin. She hadn't realized how famished she was. The nuns had given them some sandwiches for the first part of their journey, but those were long gone.

They ate in silence. Then Marcel pulled his back-pack over and turned it upside down, emptying the contents onto the hay. He reached inside and lifted a flap at the very bottom to reveal a pocket sewn into the seams. It was completely undetectable. Helen watched as he opened the concealed pocket and pulled some additional documents from it. He laid these on the hay in front of them. When Helen looked down, she could see that these were their original identity documents, the ones that Maman had given to Mère Supérieure the day they had arrived at the convent. A third document belonged to Albert. The red letter J that identified them as Jews was stamped on the front of each paper. It glowed in the soft light of the barn. Marcel looked up at them.

"You'll need these originals when you get across the border," he said. "But for now, I'm going to put them in a safer place."

Helen watched in amazement as he first wrapped the documents in wax paper. Then he cut several slices of baguette and placed the wrapped documents on the bread, adding layers of sliced cheese and tomato. Finally, he wrapped the bulging sandwich in the remaining waxed paper and stuffed it into his backpack. He smiled up at the children.

"If we're stopped, the Nazis will never look at the sandwich. They like to keep their uniforms spic and span. And they don't like to get their hands dirty going through food. Trust me," he added, noting the astonished look on Helen's face. "It's worked in the past."

"How many children have you smuggled to the border?" Helen asked.

He lay back on the hay, propped up on one arm, and placed a piece of straw in his mouth, chewing thoughtfully. "I've lost count," he finally said. "Perhaps a hundred. Maybe more."

A hundred!

"And they've all stayed safe?" This question came from Albert.

Marcel stared evenly, first at Albert and then back at Helen. "Every single one."

He sat up once more and pulled a worn map from his backpack, unfolding it and spreading it on top of the straw, and then motioning for the children to gather round.

"Let me show you where we'll be going," he said.

He placed his finger on the map to show where they were and began to trace a line to the border, through a mountain range and near towns called Meximieux and Poncin, places that Helen had never heard of before.

"It will take about six days to get to the Swiss border, possibly more, depending on how fast we can walk,"

Marcel continued. "We'll travel only at night, sleeping wherever we can during the day. We have to be as quiet as mice when we walk," he added, looking at Henry with a smile. "As quiet as Henry used to be."

Her brother smiled shyly. Helen gazed down at the map. The distance they would travel was no more than an inch or two on paper. But that small expanse would take so long to cross and cover a terrain that was unfamiliar and probably as hard as last night's hike had been—maybe harder. She swallowed and looked up at Marcel.

"And there's one more thing," he said. "There is one signal that I'll give you if there's any danger. It looks like this." That's when he held his hand up in front of them. "If you see me do this"—he twirled his pointer finger in the air in a quick succession of circles—"then you have to jump into any bush that's close to you, or behind a big tree, or in any deep rut that you see. Don't hesitate, not even for a second. Find a hiding place that is close and stay perfectly still. It's the signal that soldiers may be close by."

There was complete silence in the barn. Helen felt her heart rate quicken.

"Do you have any questions?" he asked.

"What if we do all that and we're still found?" Helen asked, her voice hoarse and shaky.

"You are a group of scouts and I am your scout-master," Marcel replied. "We're on a hike in the woods, designed to teach you survival skills and make you strong." He stared evenly at Helen. "If we're ever questioned, and I don't believe we will be, then I will do the talking. I'm counting on you to follow my directions. Any other questions?"

Helen gulped. She still had a million: How would they be able to walk for six days or more? Where would they find food? What if someone got hurt? She didn't even know where to start asking. Albert looked pale next to her but remained silent. But when she glanced over at Henry, she could see that he had a calm and determined look in his eyes. Finally, she looked back at Marcel and shook her head.

"Good," he said. "Then sleep some more and we'll be off as soon as it's dark."

And with that, he turned away and lay down.

Helen eased her body back down onto the hay and closed her eyes, wondering if she would ever be able to calm herself enough to sleep again.

CHAPTER 30

Henry

The second night of hiking felt harder than the first. The ground had become rockier and less stable, and the muscles in Henry's legs were burning. In the dark, it was hard to see where to place your foot. One wrong step and you could twist an ankle or worse—break something. Henry had already fallen a couple of times. He had a bloody scrape on one knee and a long gash down the other leg. But he refused to show how painful the cuts were, even when the clown dabbed at them with a strong-smelling liquid that he pulled from his backpack.

"Are you okay to keep going?" he asked when he paused to attend to Henry's cuts.

The antiseptic burned when it touched Henry's skin. He bit his lower lip so he wouldn't cry out. Then he looked at Helen, who hovered above him. Even in the darkness, he could see the concern glowing from her eyes. He quickly looked away. "I'm fine," he said. Then he pulled himself up from the ground and set off again.

It didn't help that the clown kept a furious pace, swerving around trees and dodging between bushes as if he were the wind itself moving through the forest. It took every ounce of Henry's strength just to keep up with him.

At the same time, Henry had to admit that there was something comforting about being in the woods. The trees reached their long branches down and practically hugged him. Leaves tickled his face as he walked by. Twigs popped and crackled under his feet. It was quiet here, just like the quiet he had grown so accustomed to back at the convent. He wasn't afraid.

Suddenly, up ahead, the clown raised his hand. He slowed to a stop and turned to wait for Henry and the others to catch up. They gathered around him. Henry was breathing heavily. The clown, on the other hand, had hardly broken a sweat. He leaned forward to talk to the group.

"It's not time to stop yet. But this is a good place for a break."

From the darkness that still surrounded him, as well as the position of the moon in the sky, Henry guessed that it would still be a couple of hours before daybreak. But he was glad for the opportunity to rest. He fell onto the forest floor and peeled his bag off his back. Then he rested his head against it. Helen and Albert looked equally relieved to sit. The clown crouched in front of them.

"There's a town close by. I need to go and meet someone there."

Henry raised his head. Who could the clown possibly have to meet in the middle of the night?

"I want the three of you to wait here for me," the clown continued. "Stay hidden. Don't move and don't come out until I come back."

Henry wasn't sure he liked the sounds of that. He didn't want the clown to leave them, even for a few minutes. Besides, he was curious. As the clown began to rise and walk away, Henry was on his feet, trotting after him. The clown turned to face him.

"What is it, Henry?"

"I don't want you to go," he said.

The clown gazed at him. "Are you afraid to be on your own?"

Henry paused and then nodded ever so slightly.

"No need for fear. I promise I'll be back before

you know it. I haven't let you down yet, have I?" He smiled as he said this.

Henry nodded again. But as the clown turned to go, Henry grabbed his arm. The clown turned and stared at Henry, and Henry stared back.

And then the clown asked, "Do you want to come with me?"

"Yes."

The clown turned to Helen and Albert. When Henry followed his glance, he could see how frightened Helen looked. Her eyes had grown wide, and she started to protest when the clown stopped her.

"You know I wouldn't put Henry in any situation that might be dangerous. He'll be fine." Then he turned back to Henry.

"Okay, my friend. I said you could be my assistant and here's your chance."

And then, the clown started off through the forest, with Henry close behind him. They walked quickly and soon emerged from the woods onto a narrow road that led directly into a small town. As they approached the main square, the clown turned to Henry and whispered, "Stay close to me. Act normal. Follow my directions."

Henry didn't know the name of this small and sleepy town. It was still quite dark outside, and most of the people who lived here were probably still fast asleep in their cozy beds. Several shopkeepers were just beginning to turn on lights in their stores. A man from the bakery opened his door and began to sweep dust and leftover crumbs onto the street. He glanced at Henry and the clown, but paid them little attention as they walked past at a casual pace. A couple of early morning street vendors were pushing their wagons onto the main square. One vendor had his wagon piled high with apples that threatened to fall as the cart lurched and swayed onto the street. Henry gazed longingly at the fruit. The clown caught his gaze but didn't stop. He clearly knew where he was headed, and he walked confidently toward a small building at one end of the square that looked like an abandoned rooming house. He paused at the door, looking in both directions. And then, he grabbed Henry by the arm and pushed him through the entrance, following close behind.

Inside, it was completely quiet. The clown steered Henry down an empty hallway, toward a room at the end where a soft glow of light was beckoning them. Henry's heart was pounding in his chest, not from fear but from excitement. Every nerve in his body was ignited with energy and anticipation. He felt as if he were on a secret mission—just him and the clown. At the end of the hallway, with one last backward glance,

the clown pushed Henry into the room, entered behind him, and shut the door tightly.

Inside the room was another young man standing
in a corner, away from the windows and partly hidden
by a tall cabinet. The man stepped out of the shadow
as Henry and the clown walked toward him.

"Marcel!" the young man exclaimed.

The clown grabbed the man in a quick hug and
then pulled away. He turned to Henry. "I'd like you to
meet Alain," he said. "My brother."

Henry stared curiously at the young man. He had
never thought about the possibility that the clown
had a brother. But here he was. And this person had
the same wiry, dark hair and the same long nose.
There was no doubting their relationship.

"He's my younger brother," the clown added,
smiling and nudging Alain playfully.

"Yes," Alain replied. "But I'm the one who's much
smarter." Then he turned to Henry and held out his
hand. "Very nice to meet you."

Henry took the extended hand and shook it. "Are
you a … a partisan, too?"

Alain smiled. "Yes. I'm doing the same kind of
work as my brother."

"Henry's my helper. But he's also a budding mime
artist," the clown added. "He understands the value
of silence."

Alain looked thoughtful. "The two of you must get along really well."

"We do," the clown replied.

In that moment, in the quiet dimness of that small room, Henry could not have felt more proud.

The two brothers talked for a few minutes. They discussed the position of Nazi troops patrolling the area and the children who were being smuggled to the border. It seemed that Alain was also helping those who were trying to get to safer places. Henry watched the exchange, soaking in every word.

"I have three with me this time," the clown said.

"I'm just back from the border," Alain replied. "I had four."

"Any trouble?"

"Nothing to worry about. We managed to avoid a couple of patrols."

"And what's next?" the clown asked.

"I have another group of four waiting for me to take them across. It seems as if our work is never done."

At that, the clown sighed and nodded. Finally, Alain reached into a bag he was carrying and pulled out a stack of papers. When Henry looked closer, he could see that they were identity papers like the one he carried in his own backpack. But these were blank;

there were no names and no photographs on them. The clown caught Henry's curious stare.

"These will enable more young people like you and your sister and Albert to move from place to place more safely. I'll fill in the blank spaces when the need arises."

With that, he reached into his backpack and placed the blank papers in the hidden compartment at the bottom.

"Thank you, Alain," he said.

The two brothers hugged once more.

"Good to meet you," Alain said, shaking hands again with Henry. "You're in good hands with my brother." He looked up at the clown. "I hear there may be troops patrolling nearby. Stay safe."

"And you, too," the clown replied.

With that, Alain left, closing the door behind him. A few minutes later, Henry and the clown followed. Before leaving the village, the clown bought four apples from the vendor in the street. He tossed one to Henry as the two of them headed out of the village and back to the woods.

Chapter 31

Helen

Three days into their journey, and the milk, baguettes, cheese, and tomatoes from the farmer's hayloft were a distant memory—as were the apples that Marcel had brought back for them after his trip to the village with Henry. Food had become scarce, and they ate mainly berries and small roots that they scavenged. They drank fresh water from small streams that flowed next to their path.

Just before daylight, Marcel sent Helen and Albert out to look for something to eat, warning them to stay within a short distance of the camp he had set up in the forest. Albert was just up ahead of her, pushing back tree branches and searching for things that he knew were edible. He held a bundle of plants in one hand and called back over his shoulder, "There are lots of weeds that we can eat. Clover is pretty good, too. And there's nectar in the flowers of some of these plants that's delicious."

"How do you know all this?" Helen asked, peering at the thick bush. Nothing looked particularly appetizing.

Albert looked over at her and smiled. "My family used to go camping all the time. My father would send us into the woods to find food, 'in case we're ever stranded on an island,' he used to say. I never thought any of that would come in handy. But I guess I have my parents to thank for this."

Albert stared off into the distance. He rarely spoke about his family.

"Do you think about them a lot? Your parents?" Helen asked.

"I used to think about them more," Albert said. "But lately, not so much. It's not that I've given up hope of ever seeing them again, it's just that I don't want to set myself up to be disappointed. And I don't want to forget about them, but remembering sometimes hurts too much."

Helen swallowed hard. "Sometimes I worry that my parents may not be coming back. I try to stop myself from thinking about that, but it isn't always possible. And then the other day, when Henry went off with Marcel to that town, it felt like forever until they got back. I kept thinking about what it would be like to lose him—to be all alone."

Albert nodded. "That's how I feel most days. You probably can't see it, and I try to stay positive, but I can't always do that." His shoulders sagged.

Helen stared at him. "Come on," she finally said. "Show me what plants to look for. We'll get a few more and then get back. Marcel told us not to wander too far."

She glanced around. They had already gone farther than they should have, and it was growing lighter by the minute. Marcel and Henry were nowhere to be seen. She and Albert would have to carefully retrace their steps to get back to their campsite.

Albert took a deep breath, shaking off the memories. Then he began to move forward. "I see a couple of plants up ahead and then we'll go—" He paused mid-sentence. A second later, he crouched down, motioning for Helen to do the same.

She ducked quickly, knowing instinctively that she needed to follow Albert's lead and ask questions later. A couple of seconds passed, and then he beckoned her to crawl forward, keep her head low. She inched up, pulling herself by her elbows along the forest floor until she was beside him. He pointed ahead.

Somehow, they had wandered to the edge of the forest. There was a small clearing just ahead, and beyond that, a village nestled into the hills. The sight of the village was not unusual. They had skirted past hamlets like this one the entire time they were hiking in the woods. Marcel had always kept them a safe distance away, warning that it was best not to be seen by anyone, even in these tiny remote communities. This village had several chalet-like houses that leaned against each another, encircling a couple of dirt roads. A church steeple rose from the center of the town. The paint on its exterior had blistered and was peeling off in chunks. Its spire tilted dangerously off its base. Ivy grew up its side unchecked. It was unusual to see a church in such disrepair. Helen knew that even the poorest communities dedicated what little money they had to keeping their churches looking like new. She was so taken with the sight of this crumbling building that for a moment, she didn't notice where Albert was pointing. And then, she saw it. In the midst of the villagers who walked along the dirt road, there were Nazi soldiers marching next to them, their rifles slung over their shoulders. Helen counted at least a dozen of them. Several held on to German shepherd dogs that drooled and strained on their leashes. They were just like the dogs she had seen the night that Papa had been taken.

Her stomach shifted uneasily, and the queasiness rose up inside of her like a gigantic wave. She swallowed hard, afraid that she might be sick right here on the edge of this village. Then she ducked her head lower and moved back into the bush, squeezing her hands up against her cheeks. They were burning hot. Albert took one look at her face, dropped the plants he had been carrying, and pulled her up to a standing position, pushing her forward through the bushes. She didn't know how they managed to make it back to the campsite.

By the time Albert finished explaining to Marcel what they had seen, Helen felt less sick, though just as anxious. "What are the Nazis doing here?" she cried. "We're in the middle of nowhere."

"It's just what your brother Alain told us," Henry said. "He said that he'd seen a Nazi patrol."

Helen hadn't known that. "Do you think this is the same group of soldiers?" she asked.

"We can't know if it's the same patrol," Marcel replied, keeping his voice even. "But we all need to remain calm. You know there are Nazis searching throughout France. That's why we're heading for the border."

Helen nodded. "But I just thought we were already far enough away ..."

"I've promised to keep you safe, and so far, no danger has come to us," Marcel continued.

So far!

"The best thing you can do"—he spread his arms wide to include Albert and Henry—"the best thing you can *all* do is get some sleep. Gather your strength. In a few days, you'll be in Switzerland and all this will be behind you."

Helen knew, even before she lay her head on the forest floor, that it would be impossible to sleep. Adrenaline pounded through her body, keeping her mind racing with thoughts of Nazi soldiers and growling German shepherds. She tossed and turned, unable to find a way to let her body relax. She sensed, from the movement in nearby bushes, that Albert and Henry were equally restless. It seemed as if hours passed like this, and then she heard Marcel get up and rouse her and the others. It was still light and Helen knew they were hours away from sunset.

When the three of them were sitting together in a circle in front of Marcel, he said, "I have a better idea."

CHAPTER 32

Henry

"We're going to do some mime," the clown said with a smile.

"Mime?" Helen asked. Henry could plainly see the look of confusion and exhaustion on her face.

Albert seemed just as confused. "You mean right now?"

"Why not?" the clown replied. "Is there something you'd rather be doing? Perhaps sleeping?"

"I think it's a good idea," Henry offered. It was obvious that they were all too anxious to sleep. He heard his sister sigh.

"There you go," the clown said. "Henry understands

that this can help take your mind off your worries, don't you, my friend?"

Henry nodded

The clown's eyes swept back over Helen and Albert. "So, are you willing to give this a try?"

The two of them nodded weakly, and the clown struck a pose in front of them. "We're all going to be waiters in an imaginary restaurant," he said. "I am a customer who doesn't like anything that he is being served." With that, the clown plopped himself down on a tree stump. He pretended to open a napkin, which he stuffed into his shirt. Then he motioned for Henry and the others to come toward him as if they were about to serve him some food. He showed them how to keep one arm bent and in front of them, as if they had a towel dangling over that arm. Helen and Albert hesitated at first, so Henry took the lead. He bent his arm and strutted up to the clown, bowing in front of him and pretending to place a platter of some kind on a make-believe table. The clown leaned forward, sniffed, wrinkled his nose, and then shoved the plate off to one side. Henry held his hands up in the air and trotted away as if he was going to get something else to serve.

It didn't take long for him to pick up the flow of the story. Though it had been some time since he had practiced the skits that the clown had taught him back at the convent, the movements came back to him easily. He shifted his body in response to the clown's actions. He reacted to every movement that the clown tossed his way with a flick of his eye, a raised brow, a startled look.

After a couple of minutes, he turned to Helen and Albert and held out his hands, inviting them to join him as waiters trying to please this difficult customer. Neither of them looked as if they wanted to try. But finally, Helen stepped forward, raised an arm and bent it in front of her, and then walked toward the clown to offer him another make-believe dish. Henry could see how awkward she was at first, forgetting that she was holding a plate and dropping her arm. He reminded her to stand straight up and keep her arm bent, no matter what. After a couple of minutes, he could see that she was getting better at following the story. He smiled at her and she grinned back.

As for Albert, he was as stiff as a post, and as clumsy as a baby learning to walk.

"I can't do this," he moaned, slumping to the forest floor and hanging his head in defeat.

"Try it again," the clown urged, breaking out of his character to talk to Albert. "You'll never get better if you give up."

Albert sighed, pulled himself to his feet, and dove back in.

They continued the story for several more minutes. The clown rejected imaginary dish after imaginary dish until finally he agreed to try something. That was when his face lit up like someone who had just gotten the best present of his life. He jumped from the tree stump and danced around in a circle. He looked so silly, kicking his heels into the air and waving his arms around his head that finally Henry couldn't control himself any longer. He fell on the ground, laughing hard and holding his sides. He could barely catch his breath. A few seconds later, Helen started to giggle. And soon after, Albert began chuckling as well. The three of them were soon howling un-controllably, losing themselves in the silliness of the moment. Henry wasn't even sure what was making him laugh until his stomach hurt. All he knew was that it felt as if he was laughing out every bit of worry he had been feeling.

All the while, he could see that the clown was watching the three of them, a big grin on his face. Finally, Henry rolled over onto his side and sat up, wiping tears from his eyes.

"You see?" the clown said. "It's the best medicine. Maybe now you'll be able to get some sleep. What do you think?"

Henry nodded and looked over at Helen and Albert. Helen's eyes, so sad before, were shining brightly.

Without another word, the three of them lay their heads back down on the forest floor. It didn't even matter that he was hungry and longing for something to eat. Henry was fast asleep within minutes. He must have slept through the rest of the day. When the clown finally woke him up, it was dark and he knew it was time to start walking again.

CHAPTER 33

Helen

Helen stumbled over some big stones and quickly regained her footing. The terrain had grown increasingly steep and rocky in the last two days of trekking. Marcel had told her they would be skirting the Jura Mountains, a mountain range that separated this part of France from Switzerland. Sometimes, they seemed to be climbing straight up, and her legs burned so much that she thought she wouldn't be able to climb anymore. But going down was even harder. Then the muscles in her thighs and calves felt like they might explode. She never said a word about how hard the hiking was, even when she felt as if she couldn't take another step. If Albert and Henry could do it, then she knew she could as well. Besides, what good would complaining do? They had to get to the border, and Marcel seemed intent on getting them there quickly, more so since she and Albert had seen those soldiers.

Thankfully, nothing bad had happened since then. The forest was peaceful, and the only sounds she heard were small animals that hunted close by and birds that flew overhead. Although the hiking was hard, Helen had even allowed herself to relax enough to imagine what it would be like when they made it to Switzerland. The first thing she would do would be to try and make contact with her mother. She didn't know how that would happen, but she would do everything in her power to find Maman and then Papa. She imagined what a happy reunion they would have. She didn't want to lose hope—couldn't lose hope. It was one of the things that kept her going through the long and tiring nights of walking.

The sky was just beginning to lighten, and she knew it was time to find a place to sleep and, hopefully, something to eat and drink. Any minute now, Marcel would raise his hand and then drop it, signaling that they could stop and rest. She couldn't wait. Her body was begging for sleep. In the dawn light, she could just make out his form walking ahead of her on the trail when suddenly, he stopped and raised his hand. But instead of dropping it, he held it in the air. They all froze.

It was then she noticed that the forest had grown quiet: no animals chucking and grunting, no birds beginning to squawk and swoop. The air felt strained and thick. Marcel seemed different as well, Helen thought—rigid, on alert, listening. Then, he turned sharply and twirled his finger in the air—a series of small, rapid circles. Helen knew what that meant. Danger!

She hesitated for only a split second and then dove into a nearby bush, only then glancing up quickly and cautiously to see where the others were. Albert was in a bush next to her, and Henry in one just ahead. Marcel had trained them well, drilled into them the need to hide immediately if they saw his emergency signal. Helen could just make out his shadowy image, crouched behind a large tree trunk and peering around to see where they were.

She heard the approaching soldiers before she saw them. There were branches crackling, a series of footsteps in a methodical marching pattern, and the unmistakable sound of German voices. Someone was barking orders.

"Search the forest," a man shouted. "There are reports of Jews in the woods. Look behind every tree and every bush. Do not overlook a thing."

Helen buried her head in her arms. Her heart was beating faster than she had ever felt before. The thumping rose into her ears and the blood pounded behind her eyes. She tried to slow her breathing, knowing she would faint if she continued to gasp for air like this. She counted her breaths in and out until, ever so slowly, she felt her breathing slow down and her heartbeat along with it.

When she lifted her head again, she looked for Albert in the bushes beside her. He glanced back at her and raised his eyebrows as if to ask if she was okay. She responded with a quick nod. Then her eyes sought out Henry in the bushes ahead of her. But instead of crouching in the undergrowth, instead of concealing himself like everyone else, instead of making himself small and undetected, Henry was up on his knees and stretching his head out toward the path where the soldiers were approaching.

Helen's heart rate began its quick climb again. Henry would be spotted if he didn't hide. He was about to put himself and everyone else in the worst possible danger. Helen wanted to shout at him to get back, lay low, cover himself with branches. But there was no way she could call out to him. She watched, the dread rising, as Henry continued to move his body out of the bushes.

But a moment later, Henry began to motion to

Marcel, raising his hand with his fingers spread—four fingers, and then a movement like a rifle raised to his shoulder, and then more fingers in the air. Could he see the soldiers when no one else could? Was he signaling the number of guns that he could detect up ahead? Or the number of soldiers coming toward them? Helen wasn't sure. But she could see that Marcel was watching Henry's movements and nodding as if he understood. Then Marcel motioned back to Henry and Henry moved his hands forward as if to show the direction that the soldiers were walking. Marcel nodded once more while Helen continued to watch in amazement. Marcel and Henry were *talking* to one another—speaking with their hands as easily as if they had been shouting.

The noises from the approaching soldiers grew louder. Dark shapes moved between the shadows of the trees. Helen caught a glimpse of a gray uniform, the flash of a red and black Nazi emblem, and the glint of a rifle butt. Branches snapped and the sound of stones being stepped on crunched in her ears. Any minute now, the soldiers would be on top of them, and then what? Would they be arrested? Shot? Tortured? The images of what might happen swirled through her head like a raging fire. Her last encounters with Nazi soldiers had frightened her. Now, she was on the brink of panic.

Up ahead, Henry was still signaling to Marcel: a change of direction, a rifle that was lowered, a re-grouping of the soldiers. Marcel signaled to Henry to move back into his bush. Suddenly, the regiment came to a stop. Now the forest was dead quiet. Helen held her breath, fearful of making even the smallest sound. That's when one of the soldiers called out, "I think I hear something up ahead." *This is it,* Helen thought. *Our journey ends here.* And then, Marcel stepped out from behind his tree and came face to face with the Nazi soldiers.

CHAPTER 34

Helen

"Halt! Arms in the air! Don't move!" The soldiers' commands shattered the silence, tumbling one on top of another as Marcel was surrounded. Helen watched, dread rising up in her throat, as he raised his hands in front of the Nazi soldiers. And then he just stood there.

"Who are you?"

"What are you doing here?"

"Answer us!"

"Stay still!"

The orders flew at him, and all the while, he just stood with his hands in the air, waiting. Finally, the noise and angry shouting died down, and one of the soldiers stepped forward to confront Marcel. "Who are you?" he demanded. "Answer me, now."

"Hello," she heard Marcel reply. Helen was amazed at how calm and composed he sounded. "You surprised me, sir. I hadn't expected to find anyone out in the woods at this early hour."

"You didn't answer my question," the soldier replied. "Who are you?"

"I'm a scoutmaster," Marcel replied. "We're from Éloise." He gestured toward a town that must have been behind them. "I have a troop of young scouts with me. We're on a hike."

The soldier was once again on guard. "Troop? How many in your troop? Where are the others?" This command was rough and loud. The soldiers trained their guns on the forest where Helen and the others were hiding.

"No need to be alarmed, sir," Marcel continued. "As I said, these are young scouts—just three of them." Then he turned and called out, "Come out of your positions. We need to talk to this soldier."

Helen couldn't believe her ears. Were they really going to reveal their hiding places? Were they going to compromise their safety? She had to trust that Marcel knew what he was doing. He had told them that if they were ever questioned, they would have to pretend to be scouts, and Marcel their scoutmaster. But in this moment, the strategy made no sense to her. She glanced over at Albert and could see that he looked equally bewildered. But when she looked forward to Henry's spot, she saw that he was already standing, had hoisted his backpack over his shoulders and was walking out of the bushes toward Marcel. Helen took a deep breath, rose, and followed.

The three children were quickly surrounded by soldiers. Helen raised her hands in the air, trying to still the trembling that had overtaken her body. Marcel stepped forward to speak once again.

"I'm teaching these young people how to survive in the elements—hunting for food, finding water and a place to sleep."

The soldier looked wary. "Why are you sneaking about this early in the morning?"

Marcel was not deterred. "I get my scouts up at the crack of dawn. I'm sure you know what it's like to teach inexperienced ones how to be strong."

The guard, who until this moment had looked intimidating and unreceptive, suddenly began to take interest in what Marcel was saying. He puffed out his chest and nodded his head. "It's like training young soldiers," he said.

"Exactly!" Marcel exclaimed. "You understand what I'm saying, sir. Strong bodies make for strong minds."

By now, the guard had lowered his rifle and was staring curiously at Marcel and at Helen, Henry, and Albert.

"I've still got a lot of work to do," Marcel continued. "The work of a scoutmaster is never done, just as your work with your soldiers continues."

That brought a broad smile to the guard's face. "I admire what you are doing," he said. "Now, if you could just show me your papers, I will let you be on your way."

Helen was astonished. Marcel had actually convinced this Nazi guard that they were equals, engaged in the same work of training recruits. Now, all they had to do was show their fake papers and they would be free to go. One by one, the children reached into their backpacks and withdrew their documents, handing them over to the guard, who took them and read them, holding them up to the dim light and then lowering them to stare at the children. Helen held her breath. Would this work? Would this soldier detect that the papers were forged? She glanced at Marcel, who scratched behind his ear and shifted from one foot to the other. He looked almost bored, waiting for the examination to end. Henry's face was passive and betrayed nothing. Meanwhile, Helen counted the seconds that passed until the guard finally lowered the papers and handed them back to the children.

"These seem to be in order," he said. Then he turned to Marcel. "If you'll just permit me to search your bag."

Marcel glanced up at the brightening sky. "We really should be on our way," he said. "We have a lot of ground to cover and I need to get these young scouts moving."

"Just a formality," the soldier insisted.

Helen's chest constricted once more as Marcel handed his backpack to the soldier, who bent, untied the strings, and began to rummage through it, pulling out a couple of sweaters and a pair of trousers before digging down to the bottom. Finally, he extracted the sandwich that Marcel had wrapped days earlier. He held it up in the air as Helen gulped once more. This was the sandwich that contained their real identity documents, concealed in waxed paper and hidden in the layers of bread, cheese, and tomato. Helen could see Marcel's hand move to the back of his belt, where he grasped the handle of the knife that he had placed there.

Meanwhile, the soldier was still examining the sandwich. And as he turned it over in his hands, some juice from the tomatoes inside escaped from the wax wrapping and dripped down on the soldier's uniform. He threw the sandwich onto the ground and rose, wiping furiously at the stain that was spreading across his trouser leg.

"My apologies, sir," Marcel said, releasing his grip on his knife. With that, he turned to Helen. "You didn't wrap this very well," he said. "Now look what you've done to this commander's uniform."

Helen's mouth gaped open. "I-I'm ... sorry," she stuttered.

Marcel turned back to the soldier. "As I said, these young scouts still have a lot to learn. Is there something I can do to help?"

The soldier was still rubbing at the stain on his uniform. He shooed away Marcel, who had taken another step forward.

"Get away from me," the soldier commanded. And then he muttered, "Disgusting," under his breath.

Marcel retreated and reached down to retrieve the sandwich. But just then, another soldier stepped forward and pushed him away. Helen froze once more as the soldier bent down and picked the soggy wrapped sandwich off the ground. He held it up in the air with one hand, careful to avoid the stream of tomato juice that was dripping from one corner. He sniffed at it, recoiled slightly, and then leaned forward to inspect it once more. Could he see the documents hidden inside? Would he unwrap the sandwich and reveal the true identities of the children? Helen's heart began to pound even more. Her eyes sought out Marcel's. His brow was knitted together and his hand once again reached behind him to grasp the handle of his knife. He stepped forward.

"Excuse me, sir," he began, bowing to the soldier who still held the sandwich in his outstretched hand. "I feel terrible that we've made such a mess of your commander's uniform. By way of apology, let me offer a bit of entertainment to you and all of the soldiers." He pointed to the children. "My young friends here are not only scouts in training, they are also young performers."

The soldier stopped inspecting the sandwich and looked up. Even their commander stopped rubbing at the stain on his uniform. "Performers?" He stared at Helen, Henry, and Albert. "What did you say your names were?"

Helen was the first one to speak. "I'm Claire Rochette," she said, trying to keep her voice even.

"Marc," Albert said next. His face had gone white. "Marc Durand."

But when Helen looked over at Henry, she could see that he was frozen. All of the courage that he had shown until now seemed to have disappeared. A veil of fear passed over his face and rested there like a thick blanket.

"And you?" the soldier said, staring at Henry. "I asked your name."

Henry opened his mouth to speak and then clamped it shut. His eyes were bulging, his breath coming in quick shallow gulps.

This can't be happening again, Helen thought. *Not now!* It was as if Henry was disappearing back into that silent place.

"Well?" the soldier insisted.

And still no sound came out of Henry. The soldier was just beginning to come closer when Helen spoke up again. "His name is Andre. He's my brother. He's very shy." It was as if they were back in the store again, Henry paralyzed with fear and Helen trying desperately to rescue him. And then she took a deep breath and said, "And yes, we're performers. Would you like to see?"

The soldier paused, his gaze shifting from Henry over to Helen.

Without waiting for a reply, Helen took a step forward and bowed deeply to the soldiers, sweeping her arm across her chest and plunging forward from the waist. She held her position until she heard the soldiers begin to chuckle. Only then did she stand up and take her position. She knew exactly which skit she would do for the soldiers. It was the very first one she had seen Marcel do at the convent—where he was the lion tamer. Helen extended her arm out in front of her, pretending to hold an imaginary chair. She thrust the chair forward and snapped her other hand in the air as if she were holding a whip. But as she tried to shuffle forward and back, she knew that her movements were clumsy and not at all convincing.

"I don't know what she's trying to do," one of the soldiers said. "Has she got a fan in her hand?"

Helen tried once more, snapping her make-believe whip and trying to command the lion to sit and then stand up on its hind legs.

The commander scratched at his head. "Perhaps it's a sword," he said.

Finally, Helen turned to face Henry. She looked him straight in the eye, urging him to join her. *I need your help, Henry,* her eyes pleaded. *Show the soldiers that you can do this.*

Henry gulped, nodded, and jumped in behind his sister. He held his own make-believe whip and chair in his hand and began to push the imaginary lion back a few steps.

"It's a lion," the soldier exclaimed. "Can't you see it?"

With Henry by her side, Helen began to force the lion to yield to her. At one point, Henry approached the lion and pretended to force it to open its mouth, placing his own head inside. The soldiers roared their approval.

The next time Helen turned around, her eyes locked with Albert's. If they were to convince these guards that they could put on a show, then all three of them would have to join in. The color had drained from Albert's face and he was breathing fast. But Helen held out her hand to him and he grabbed it. It was cold and clammy, but she held fast and pulled him into their circus ring. The three of them began to walk forward, making the imaginary lion lie down and roll over as if it were a puppy. Albert was as stiff and awkward as he had been when they had first tried the skits in the forest.

At one point, he very nearly lost his balance as he pretended that the lion was coming after him. He turned and began to run around the imaginary ring. His arms windmilled in circles as he struggled to regain his footing. Helen and Henry both reached out to grab him and pull him upright. The soldiers roared with laughter and applauded loudly. It was if Albert's clumsiness was the funniest part of the routine. And as the laughter from the guards grew, Albert began to exaggerate the awkward movements, tripping over his feet and nearly falling to the ground again. The soldiers roared even louder. Finally, the three children held their hands up in the air and bowed once more to the soldiers, who cheered.

Their commander nodded his head approvingly. "You are training them well, indeed," he said to Marcel, "and giving them many skills." He pointed at Albert. "That one is a real comedian."

Marcel responded with a bow that was as deep and dramatic as the children's had been. By now, the soldier holding the sandwich had discarded it onto the ground. Quietly and almost invisibly, Helen reached down, retrieved the sandwich, and stuffed it back into Marcel's bag.

Finally, the commander barked at his troop to fall into line. He bowed curtly to Marcel and then marched his regiment off into the forest, leaving Helen and the others alone once more. Gradually, the shouts and commands from the troop's leader grew fainter, their footfalls and popping of branches faded and finally disappeared. Birds began to fly overhead and small animals resumed their foraging. Marcel held his hand up in the air, indicating that the children should keep still and not talk for a few minutes longer, just to be sure that the danger had passed. Finally, he lowered his hand.

That was when Helen sank to the ground. She was so shaken from this encounter with the soldiers that she no longer trusted herself to remain standing.

Albert seemed just as stunned. A moment later, Henry walked over to her and crouched down. She smiled faintly at him.

"Are you all right?" Henry asked.

She reached over and brushed the curls off his forehead. He didn't flinch and he didn't move away. "I'm … I'm fine. What about you?"

He grinned. "I'm okay."

As he smiled broadly, one eyebrow lifted up higher than the other. It was just like Maman! Helen gasped. "You were amazing," she said. "Signaling to Marcel like that."

"I got scared when they spoke to me," Henry said, looking down.

"It doesn't matter. You jumped into the skit when you needed to. The important thing is that we got through it."

Henry shrugged. "You were pretty good, too. You knew what to do when the clown wanted us to perform."

By now, Albert had walked over to join them. He kneeled down beside Helen.

"And you were the biggest surprise of all," she said to him.

"Who knew that acting badly could actually be good," Albert replied, laughing softly and shaking his head.

Marcel listened to their exchange. "You were all more than amazing," he said quietly. "The three of you completely distracted the soldiers with your performance. I knew I could count on you."

CHAPTER 35

Henry

The hiking had gotten easier again. Henry felt strong as he trekked up and down those steep hills in the fresh air. He felt muscles in his legs that he hadn't felt in such a long time. His senses were more alert as well. He could tell whether the crackle of a branch was simply a rabbit scurrying up ahead or a deer stepping over a fallen tree trunk or a fox hunting for small rodents.

There had been no other encounters with the Nazis, though Henry was always on guard for any sign of trouble. When the clown had raised his hand with his danger signal, it felt like second nature to him to hide, and then to pass messages to the clown. So, he wasn't sure why he had frozen like that when the soldier had asked his name. Thank goodness Helen had stepped in. Together, they had done everything that the clown had taught them. Still, he wasn't sure what had overtaken him back there, and it troubled him.

He talked to Helen about this as they trudged through the woods.

"Were you scared?" he asked. "Back there with those soldiers? When they were talking to you?"

She looked at him. "I was very scared!"

"But you didn't look it."

Helen shrugged. "That's just an act. If you could have looked inside of me, you would have seen that I was a wreck."

Henry smiled. "I thought you said you weren't very good at acting."

This time it was Helen's turn to smile. "I guess I'm getting better."

The growth in the forest had started to thin out. Trees were farther apart and the path under Henry's feet was growing flatter and more even. Up ahead, Henry could hear something new—the sound of rushing water. A few steps farther and they were out of the woods and onto the bank of a river that stretched in both directions for as far as Henry could see. Water was flowing across rocks and logs, surging past in some places and then slowing to a lazy current in others. The clown came to a stop. A moment later, they joined him at the river's edge.

"We have to cross here," the clown said. "And then, our destination will be near."

Destination? Henry could not believe his ears. Were they really that close to the Swiss border? When he looked at Helen, her mouth had dropped open and she, too, was staring across the river in disbelief.

"You'll have to hold your backpacks above your heads as you cross," the clown continued. "It isn't too deep, but the footing can be a bit tricky. Don't worry," he added. "I'll lead the way." With that, he turned and began to wade across the river. He moved quickly until he was roughly halfway across. The water swirled around his legs and splashed up to his waist. Then he turned back to the group still standing on the bank.

"You see?" he called back. "It isn't too deep. Follow the course that I took. Come toward me and then we'll go from here."

For a moment, no one moved. And then, Albert took the first step. He lifted his backpack up in the air and waded into the water. Henry watched as he carefully picked his way to the center of the river and then glanced back, motioning for them to follow.

Helen stepped in next, carefully placing one foot in front of the other. Finally, it was Henry's turn. The water was icy cold, creeping up his legs until it came to just below his waist. He placed his feet ever so carefully on the river bottom, wobbling over some loose stones and then finding a secure footing.

"Are you okay?" Helen called back to him.

He looked up and smiled, nodding at her to keep going. "I'm fine," he replied. "Right behind you."

It took about twenty steps for Henry to reach the midpoint. When they were all together, the clown nodded his approval and then continued wading forward until he arrived at the other bank and climbed out. Then he turned once more. "You're almost there," he said. And then he motioned for Henry and the others to follow.

Minutes later, all of them stood on the opposite shore, wringing out their trousers and placing their bundles on their backs once more. The clown waited until everyone was ready before he took off, proceeding along a path and then turning sharply to the left. After a few more minutes of walking, he raised his hand. Henry and the others gathered around him. That's when the clown pointed ahead of them to a barbed-wire fence that looked nearly as high as the clown. It stretched to the right and to the left, disappearing into the distance on either side.

"That's the border," the clown said.

CHAPTER 36

Helen

When people had said that Switzerland was a safe place for Jews, Helen had thought it meant that Jews would be made to feel welcome there. But there were no open doors at the Swiss border—no signs that said "We're glad to have you." There was nothing friendly about the barbed-wire fence that looked six feet high and miles wide. It was ugly and hostile. Its razor-sharp spikes said no one was wanted.

Even worse than the fence itself were the soldiers on the other side. They patrolled back and forth, some carrying rifles on their shoulders, others pointing them directly in front of them, ready to use if provoked. Helen had thought that the soldiers would greet them warmly in this so-called safe country. That didn't look as if it was going to happen. These soldiers looked just as threatening as the Nazi soldiers they were fleeing.

As if he had read her mind, Marcel gathered the children toward him and knelt down. They crouched in front of him.

"I'll help get you past the barbed wire," he said, his voice low and urgent. "But after that, you'll be on your own."

Helen glanced nervously at the soldiers.

"I know," Marcel said. "They don't look friendly. They've caught too many spies trying to get across. They'll be suspicious of you, even though you're young. That's why you'll have to show them these."

With that, he reached into his backpack and pulled out the sandwich that he had wrapped days earlier. It was flattened from having been banged about in his bag and inspected by the Nazi soldier. It looked soft and soggy. He placed the sandwich on the ground before him and slowly unwrapped it. Then he peeled off the top of the baguette and removed the documents wrapped and hidden inside. Then he unwrapped those, being careful not to let them get wet, and smiled.

"I knew those soldiers would never get to these. Good thing they were protected by the wax paper."

He held the papers up in the air.

"Clean as a whistle," he said, handing Helen, Henry, and Albert their identity documents. "Keep these in your pockets. As soon as the soldiers surround you, tell them who you are and show them your papers. You'll be fine."

Helen looked down at hers. Her real name—Helen Rosenthal—was spelled out in dark letters. She hoped she would never have to use that other name again.

"I have one more thing for you," Marcel said, glancing at Helen and Henry.

They both watched as he reached into his bag again and pulled out another soggy sandwich that had been buried at the bottom. He unwrapped it and pulled the layers apart to reveal what looked like one more document, still wrapped up. And when he pulled the waxy layers away, Helen realized what it was. She gasped when she saw the two small photographs of her parents that Marcel had pulled out of her backpack before they left the convent—her father, so serious and unsmiling, and Maman, her eyes lit up and that one freckle by the side of her mouth.

"How did you manage to keep these?" Helen asked in amazement.

"I knew they were too important to leave behind. I wrapped them up that first day in the barn, just like your documents."

Gently, the clown placed the photos in Helen's hands. She stared down at them for a moment, then smoothed them out and brought them close to her body. Even though there were tears in her eyes, she looked up at Marcel and smiled.

"Once the Swiss government is convinced you are not a threat, they'll help you try and find your parents," he said softly "You can't lose hope."

"Thank you," she said, her voice catching.

Marcel glanced up at the sky and then once more at the barbed-wire fence. "We'll wait for the soldiers to change guard and then we'll dig our way under the fence." He looked back at Helen, Henry, and Albert with a smile. "Are you ready to get dirty?"

All three children nodded.

CHAPTER 37

Henry

Once the soldiers finished their shift, they would disappear inside the barrack. Then, the clown explained, they would have only ten minutes to dig a hole and burrow under the fence before new soldiers came on duty. They would have to work quickly. But the clown told Henry and the others that before that could happen, they should rest and gather their strength for what would be their final push to safety.

Henry removed his backpack and rested his head against it. That's when Helen crawled over to where he was lying. Henry sat up.

"I just wanted to make sure you're okay," she said as she sat cross-legged in front of him.

Henry picked at a thread that dangled from his pack. "You're always doing that."

"Doing what?"

"Making sure I'm okay."

"I guess I can't help myself," Helen said. "You're my little brother. Maman told me to watch out for you."

"She said we should watch out for each other," Henry said.

Helen nodded. "You're right. I guess you're a lot stronger than I thought."

"Maman told me I had to be brave," Henry continued. "She wrote that in her letter to me."

That's when Henry told Helen about going to the zoo with Maman and Papa, and about how he had wanted to put his hand inside the lion's cage, thinking he could tame the wild animal. "Maman wrote that if I ever felt scared, I should think about that time."

"I remember that!" Helen exclaimed. "Maman and Papa were so afraid for you. But you were fearless." She paused. "I won't underestimate you anymore, Henry."

"You're pretty brave yourself," he replied, still picking at the thread. "And I don't mind if you look out for me every now and then."

"As long as you do the same for me."

Just then, Henry detected some movement on the

other side of the barbed wire. The soldiers were falling into a straight line and marching toward the small building that was their outpost. The clown was by their side in an instant.

"Now's our chance," he said, motioning for the three children to crawl after him to the fence.

They followed on hands and knees and immediately began to dig in the soft dirt, taking turns until they had made a deep ditch. Then the clown removed his jacket and used it to raise the barbed wire up so that it wouldn't brush against their backs when they wiggled underneath.

Albert was the first to go. He shook hands with the clown and thanked him over and over for all his help. Then he fell to his stomach and slid into the ditch and under the wire. He crouched on the other side and looked back, waiting.

Helen was next. At first, she hesitated.

"I-I don't know how ... I'm not sure what ..."

The clown brushed her stammers aside. "You found your strength in the forest. Don't lose it. Just stay safe. That's all the thanks I need."

Helen nodded and then threw herself at the clown, hugging him tightly before she finally pulled away.

Without another word, the clown held the barbed wire up for Helen to slither under.

And finally, it's was Henry's turn.

For a moment, he didn't want to leave. He wanted to stay with the clown, as much as he knew he had to be with his sister and Albert.

"You really must begin to call me Marcel," the clown began. "We're friends now. We've been through a lot together, haven't we?" he added.

Henry nodded and smiled. "Marcel." It sounded strange in his mouth. This man would always and forever be simply the clown to him. "Thank you," he said, and then he flew into the clown's arms, hugging him with all his strength, not wanting to let go.

The clown finally pulled Henry's arms from around him and leaned forward to look him in the eyes.

"Practice hard, my young friend," he said. "Perhaps we'll meet again when all of this madness has passed. You can show me everything that you've learned in the meantime."

Henry nodded and wiped at the tears pooling in his eyes. Then he took a deep breath and scurried under the wire to join the others.

CHAPTER 38

Helen

No sooner had they all stood up on the Swiss side of the border than they were surrounded by soldiers.

"Halt! Show your hands." Loud voices shouted at them.

Helen raised her arms into the air. Henry and Albert did the same. Albert was the first to speak.

"We have papers," he exclaimed. "They're in our pockets. Can we show them to you?"

These soldiers did not look as if they were going to give them a chance to explain or show anything. They continued to wave their rifles in the children's faces, ordering them to stand still, raise their hands, not say a word. The soldiers wore long green jackets, tightened at the waist with thick brown belts. Helen couldn't see their faces for the bowl-shaped helmets that were pulled low over their eyes. But everything about them reminded her of the Nazis who had surrounded them in the forest on the other side. These guards, with their guns leveled at the spot between her eyes, were terrifying.

Albert was still talking, explaining that they were Jewish children from one of the convents in France. Helen finally chimed in. "If you'll just let me," she begged, "I'm going to reach into my pocket and pull out my documents." Even to her own ears, her voice was remarkably calm and strong.

The soldiers hesitated, staring at the children and then at each other. Finally, one of them nodded at Helen. Slowly and carefully, she reached into her pocket and pulled out her paper. She held it out to the soldier, who grabbed it and then lowered his rifle to rest against his leg. A moment later, he nodded to Helen. She turned to Henry and Albert and said, "Okay. Show them your papers."

She watched as Henry reached down and pulled his identity document from his pocket. Albert did the same. They extended these to the soldier, who grabbed them as well. He brought the three documents up close to his face, squinting to see what was written, and then lowering the papers to compare the photographs to the children standing in front of him. The red letter J glowed from the top of each document. While this soldier inspected their papers, the others continued to point their rifles at the children.

Back and forth the soldier went, first to the papers, then to the children, then down to the papers again. Helen was beginning to squirm. She could feel a line of sweat gathering just above her eyebrows. But she didn't want to show these soldiers that she was afraid. Marcel was right. She had found her strength back in France. She knew what to do if danger was about. She willed herself to remain calm and she stared evenly at the soldiers.

Finally, after what felt like an eternity, the soldier looked up once again. This time, he seemed more relaxed. He pushed his helmet to the back of his head to reveal his eyes. They seemed warm and maybe just a bit welcoming. When he picked up his rifle again, he didn't point it at Helen and the others. He simply slung it over his shoulder. The other soldiers followed his lead. Then he turned toward the small building and motioned for Helen and the others to follow. Albert went first, with Henry close behind.

Helen turned back once more to glance across the barbed wire to the French side. She wasn't sure what it was that she was looking for—a last wave from Marcel? A signal of some kind? There was nothing. Everything was quiet across the border. The trees were still, their branches fluttering slightly with the wind. Then suddenly, something caught her eye—a small movement in the bushes. Helen paused and squinted. A moment later, Marcel emerged from where he had been hiding in wait to see that they were safe.

Helen's face broke into a wide grin. She raised her arm to wave at Marcel. He smiled and then brought his hands together in front of him. As Helen watched, he placed one hand on top of the other and began to move them both up and down, rolling them like waves on the sea. Helen had watched him do this exact movement when he was teaching Henry back at the convent. Marcel's hands were transforming into a bird, with wings that were spread wide. The bird continued to swoop up and down, and then, as Helen watched, Marcel stretched his hands high into the air and released the bird, letting it take flight and soar— free at last.

Helen followed the imaginary bird up into the sky. Then her eyes came back to rest on Marcel, who turned and disappeared back into the bushes.

Catching up with Henry, she put an arm around his shoulder. He leaned into her, and together, they walked onward.

Who Was Marcel Marceau?

Marcel Marceau was born Marcel Mangel in 1923 in Strasbourg, France, the son of a Jewish butcher. His father introduced him to music and movies at a very young age. When he was only five years old, he saw a film with Charlie Chaplin, the American silent film actor. Marcel was fascinated that someone could entertain an audience without saying a word. He was determined that he would grow up to entertain people in the same way.

Marcel was only ten years old when Adolf Hitler came to power and began to introduce laws and rules to restrict the freedom of Jewish people. Conditions worsened until September 1, 1939, when Germany under Hitler invaded Poland to begin the Second World War. On the same day, the Jews of Marcel's city were ordered to pack their belongings for transport to a labor camp in southern France. Marcel was sixteen years old when he and his younger brother, Alain, fled from Strasbourg and joined the French Resistance. Marcel changed his last name to Marceau after a famous general of the French Revolution.

Marcel was skilled at forging identity cards, and he began to smuggle Jewish children who were hiding in convents and orphanages in southern France to the Swiss border. He pretended to be a scoutmaster leading a group of campers on hikes. He often used mime to keep the young children quiet and calm. And he sometimes concealed their real identity documents in sandwiches slathered with mayonnaise, knowing the soldiers would never want to risk dirtying their uniforms by handling the mushy sandwiches. He and the other members of his Resistance group are credited with saving the lives of hundreds of Jewish children.

When the war ended, Marcel discovered that while his mother had survived, his father had been killed in the concentration camp called Auschwitz. He began to study mime seriously by enrolling as a student in the School of Dramatic Art in Paris. It was there that he invented his most famous mime character, a white-faced clown named Bip who wore a tall hat with a red flower. He began to tour around the world as Bip.

In 1959, he created his own school in Paris and established the Marceau Foundation to promote the art of mime in the United States. He wrote several books and appeared on the stage and in film. He never spoke about his Jewish background, the death of his father, or what he had done to help save Jewish children, although later in his life, he acknowledged that the character of Bip was a tribute to all those who had been silenced in the concentration camps of Europe.

In April 2001, Marcel was awarded the Raoul Wallenberg Medal in recognition of his acts of courage aiding Jews during the Second World War. In accepting the award, Marcel said, "I don't like to speak about myself, because what I did humbly during the war was only a small part of what happened to heroes who died through their deeds in times of danger."[1]

Marcel Marceau died in September 2007 at the age of eighty-four. He was known as the Master of Silence, and was one of the greatest mime artists of all time.

---

1. Ronda Robinson. "Marcel Marceau Saved Hundreds of Holocaust Orphans." www.aish.com/jw/s/Marcel-Marceau-Saved-Hundreds-of-Holocaust-Orphans.html

ACKNOWLEDGMENTS

This story was a "gift" to me from Rick Wilks. I'm so grateful to have been given the opportunity to write a book focusing on the life of Marcel Marceau, and I'm thankful for this chance to work with Rick and the wonderful people at Annick Press. Yours is truly a first-class publishing house. I'm looking forward to diving into the next two books in the Heroes Quartet series.

Barbara Berson was a great editor for this story—insightful, thorough, and patient with me as I struggled through the needed changes. Thanks so much for helping guide the manuscript.

As always, to my husband, Ian Epstein, and my children, Gabi Epstein and Jake Epstein; your love, laugher, and encouragement sustain me.

Kathy Kacer is the author of more than twenty books for young readers. A winner of the Silver Birch, Red Maple, and Jewish Book Awards in Canada and the U.S., Kathy has written unforgettable stories inspired by real events. She lives in Toronto, Ontario.